OUTLAW RIDGE: AIDEN

Delores Fossen

Lone Star Books

Copyright © 2025 Delores Fossen

All rights reserved

The characters and events portrayed in this book are fictitious. Any similarity to real persons, living or dead, is coincidental and not intended by the author.

No part of this book may be reproduced, or stored in a retrieval system, or transmitted in any form or by any means, electronic, mechanical, photocopying, recording, or otherwise, without express written permission of the publisher.

ISBN-978-1-965032-11-4
Library of Congress Control Number: 2018675309
Printed in the United States of America

To Luke, Ruth and Finley. You'll always have my heart.

CHAPTER ONE

———— ☆ ————

There was blood on the wedding dress.

That was the first thing Deputy Lexa Mullen noticed when she stepped into the room. A crescent-shaped swath of the bright red spatter was across the ivory silk. But there were plenty of other things in the room that soon caught her attention.

Along with putting a huge knot in her gut.

The dress was lying in a crumpled heap on the floor, making it look like a headless, limbless body. The shoes were there, too. Pearl studded heels, also streaked with blood.

In fact, there were streaks and spatters everywhere in the changing room of the wedding hall. On the ceiling, the walls, the large shoulder purse sitting on a chair, and there was a plate-sized puddle of it on the floor.

What the hell had happened here?

It definitely wasn't just a break-in that the cleaning lady, Esther Drummond, had reported when she'd shown up for duty and found the front door of the wedding venue, the Yellow Rose Manor, wide open. That's when the woman had seen several smashed vases, crushed artificial flowers, and overturned chairs.

Thankfully, Esther hadn't gone inside to check things out but had instead called Outlaw Ridge PD. Since Lexa was on the swing shift and on her way back from her dinner break, she'd responded solo, figuring it would turn out to be a prank by bored school kids on summer vacation.

But this was no prank.

The blood was real. Lexa was familiar with the metallic scent, a skillset she'd unfortunately acquired from being a cop for nearly a dozen years. During those first eleven and a half years in San Antonio PD, she had encountered several bloody, grisly scenes. But in a small town like Outlaw Ridge, it wasn't a usual occurrence.

Well, it hadn't been until four months ago when most of the town's police force had been murdered. But that killer had been caught and was, thankfully, now dead. He definitely hadn't been responsible for this carnage.

So who had done this?

Checking around her, she took out her phone and sent the code for backup and also fired off a text to request a CSI team. It wouldn't take long for one of the other four swing shift deputies to show because the police station was just six blocks away on Main Street. The CSIs though might not be here for a half hour or so which meant she needed to secure the scene and check for a survivor.

And a possible killer.

Lexa put away her phone, and making sure she didn't step in any of the blood, she made her way around the room to a tall, old-fashioned wardrobe in the corner. The double doors were open just a sliver, and while she didn't hear anyone moving around in there, the furniture piece was plenty big enough for someone to use it as a hiding place.

Or a place to stash a body.

Keeping her gun ready, Lexa used her left hand to throw open the door, her entire body braced for an attacker. But the bracing wasn't necessary. Because other than a dozen or so black umbrellas, it was empty.

Lexa made her way to the purse, and she could see a blood spattered wallet inside it. She yanked out a plastic glove from her pocket, snapped it on and had a look.

Her heart dropped when she saw the driver's license.

Because it belonged to Chloe Adams, AKA the bride. Or rather the woman who would soon be the bride since the wedding was the day after tomorrow, scheduled to take place right here in this very building.

Lexa knew Chloe. Of course, that applied to just about everyone in such a small town like Outlaw Ridge. She didn't know Chloe that well though since she'd only been in town for about six months, and Lexa herself had only recently moved back to accept the deputy position. But Lexa knew the groom, Brady Kern, since they'd graduated high school together.

Soon, she'd have to talk to him. Soon, Lexa would need to find out if Brady knew what had gone on here. For now though, she needed to wait for backup, continue to examine the scene, and more importantly, try to find the person who'd lost all this blood.

Maybe Chloe.

But Chole's car wasn't outside. No one's other than Esther's had been there, so all this blood could be from someone else. Perhaps the person who'd broken in. He or she could have had a really bad encounter with...hell, a killer. Lexa didn't think it was her imagination that it was a fatal amount of blood around the room.

She made her way to the door, and she brought up her gun again when she heard the footsteps. And the voice.

"It's me," a man called out.

Aiden Brodie.

She silently groaned. Why hadn't one of the other deputies responded? Why did it have to be him? Lexa shoved aside the uneasiness. The memories. And the unwanted swirl of heat that came whenever she was around Aiden.

"Back here," she let him know.

She heard the thud on his boots on the old wood floor. Not cowboy boots but rather steeled toes combat ones, probably a holdover from his days in military special ops.

Because she'd read the background on him, Lexa knew that Aiden had had a decorated career as a Navy SEAL before he'd left the service and become an operative for Strike Force, an elite security company owned by hometown hero, Owen Striker. These days though Owen not only ran Strike Force but also pulled duty as the acting sheriff until a replacement could be hired.

This definitely wasn't the first time that Aiden's and her paths had crossed. Nope. He wasn't local, but three years ago, they'd had an *encounter*.

God, what a sterile word for something that was far from sterile.

An encounter that'd happened when he'd been tracking down an eighteen-year-old girl who'd been kidnapped by her estranged boyfriend. The girl's parents had been friends of Owen's and had requested Strike Force's assistance. That assistance had come in the form of Aiden in full Navy SEAL mode and Strike Force's massive resources that had helped him locate the girl and her ex within hours.

As a homicide detective in San Antonio PD, Lexa had been on the couple's trail, too, since the boyfriend had murdered the girl's current guy and he was in her jurisdiction. Following her own leads and using her own resources, Aiden and she had shown up at the remote campsite within minutes of each other.

And it hadn't gone well at all.

It had ended with a nightmare.

Lexa got a slam of those nightmarish images now and had to punch them aside again. She couldn't deal with that now. Not when she had to do a different kind of steeling up with him.

Aiden stepped in the doorway, and Lexa cursed the little flutter she got in her stomach at seeing him. All that black hair, green bedroom eyes, and a face that had clearly gotten the best of the best in his gene pool.

She hated that quivering sensation. Hated the reaction, especially now. It seemed disrespectful in what was a crime scene. Yet, there it was, a flutter fueled by this incredibly hot guy who seemed to have her hormonal number. The yen to that yang was that he also triggered those memories. Those nightmares.

So, yeah, it was the very definition of a complicated relationship when it came to Aiden and her.

"Jesus," he muttered, putting his hands on his hips. No uniform for him. Well, not a cop's unform anyway. He was wearing his usual dark camo pants and a black tee.

She watched as his gaze swept around the room, taking in the dress, the blood, the still-open wardrobe, and the purse.

"Is that Chloe's bag?" he asked. Like Lexa, he'd known the woman for the handful of months that he'd been on the force. He knew the groom, too, since they'd not only once served together, they were still friends.

Lexa nodded. "It's Chloe's bag. We need to look around, and then I'll call Brady. It's possible there's someone injured nearby." *Nearby* because she couldn't fathom anyone getting too far after losing that much blood.

Aiden made a sound of agreement and followed her out into the hall and to the other rooms located here. They turned on lights along the way, checking the floor for blood.

And she saw some.

Not a puddle like in the changing room but there were some drops, and Aiden and she were careful not to step in them.

They came to a closed door, and according to the nameplate on the wall, it was the office for the owner, Lily Whitaker. It was locked up tight, but the next room was open. It was a large meeting area with whiteboards filled with photos that appeared to be showcasing weddings, flower arrangements, and decorations. It was very much empty, and she couldn't see any blood in there.

"Chloe?" she called out.

No one answered, and that sense of dread that was already crawling through Lexa got a whole lot worse.

Behind her, she heard Aiden texting someone, and a couple of moments later, he whispered, "No one's come into the ER or been admitted to the hospital tonight."

Lexa was glad he'd checked so they could rule that out, and they kept moving. Kept looking, but

Lexa didn't spot any more blood.

They threaded their way to the main part of the wedding venue where there were a dozen rows of empty seats on each side. The fifty-something-year-old cleaning woman, Esther, was still there in the entry, right where Lexa had left her. Again, she was someone Lexa knew since her late mother and Esther had once been friends.

"Did you find the little shits who broke those vases and messed up the place?" Esther asked, clearly peeved at the vandalism.

Lexa shook her head. "Did you see or hear anyone when you got here?"

"Just that." Esther threw her hand in the direction of the shattered glass and flower debris on the floor. "But there could be more. Is there more?" she pressed, swinging her attention between Aiden and Lexa.

Lexa went with a question of her own. "Did you know there's a wedding dress in the changing room?"

The woman gave a quick nod. "Yeah, the boss lady told me to be careful when I cleaned in there, that she'd given Chloe a key and she was going to bring her dress over. Apparently, it's too poofy for Chloe to sit in a car for the drive over so she's getting ready here."

A key, Lexa mentally repeated, but she didn't question why Lily Whitaker had done that. It was the sort of thing that happened in a small town, and Lily was good friends with the groom's father and late mother. Still, Lexa could question the timing of events. Had Chloe used the key to bring in the dress and then left, perhaps accidentally leaving the door open?

"What about the lock?" Aiden asked, motioning toward the door. "That's a double-keyed deadbolt. It looks fairly new."

"It is," Esther verified. "The boss lady had it installed about four months ago after that shithead killed all those cops." She stopped, muttered something that Lexa didn't catch and crossed herself. "She got spooked about working in here alone, sometimes way late at night, and about so many people having keys to the place. So, if she locks it from inside while she's working, no one's getting in even if they have a key to the outside lock."

That made sense. And Lexa hated to admit it, but she'd gotten spooked, too, about those cop murders, and she had installed a security system once she'd moved back to Outlaw Ridge.

"I gotta get this place cleaned up," Esther grumbled, her expression going sour when she eyed the mess on the floor again. "The wedding's in two days, and I've got other jobs all lined up for tomorrow."

"I'm sorry, but you can't clean." Lexa paused, trying to choose her words carefully. She definitely didn't want Esther gossiping about this before Aiden and she had had a chance to keep looking for a body. "There's been some damage in the changing room, and it needs to be investigated."

Esther's eyes widened. "What did those little shits do?"

Again, Lexa didn't respond to that. "Esther, I need you to drop by the police station and give a statement. I'll contact Lily and let her know what's going on."

The woman's mouth tightened. "I hope you find those little shits, lock 'em up and throw away the key. Please don't tell me this is gonna mess with the wedding."

"I can't say," Lexa answered honestly.

Cursing under her breath and tossing out liberal amounts of *little shits*, Esther turned and lumbered her way to her car.

"We need to check the rest of the building," Aiden said. "There are restrooms and a kitchen on that side." He motioned to the right. "Hayes and Jemma are getting married here in the spring, and they had me come with them to look at the place."

No need for her to ask who they were. Hayes was his brother and a member of Strike Force, and Jemma was a fellow deputy. The two had gotten engaged a month ago.

"Do you have Brady's number?" Lexa asked Aiden as they started toward the section they hadn't checked.

He nodded and took out his phone again. "I won't mention the blood," Aiden assured her, and he hit the man's number in his contacts. Because he'd put it on speaker, Lexa heard it ring.

And then go to voicemail.

Aiden didn't leave a message. He hit end call and looked at her. "I don't have Chloe's number. Do you?"

"No. But I can go through dispatch." Lexa started that process while she continued to listen for any sounds and look for more blood.

She was still on hold with dispatch when they reached the kitchen that gleamed with stainless steel appliances and work surfaces. Nothing seemed out of place here. Not at first anyway. But she saw Aiden make a beeline to a knife storage block.

"The butcher knife's missing," he muttered, checking the sink and the dishwasher. It wasn't in either of those places.

"Call going through to Chloe now," the dispatcher said.

There was a slight click, followed by a ring. Lexa didn't just hear it on the end of the line though.

She heard it in the building.

Aiden's head whipped up, and he turned in the direction of the sound that was coming from the women's bathroom. Definitely a phone. They took off toward it, hurrying but then slowing as they approached the door. Aiden moved to one side and Lexa to the other. He mouthed the countdown of *one, two, three.*

And they burst into the bathroom.

Lexa took in the area with a cop's glance. The

sinks and mirrors The three open doors of the toilet stalls. The cell phone lying on the floor.

The blood.

More spatter was on the walls, but what caught her attention were the drag marks. Or maybe crawl marks. It was hard to tell, but the blood was smeared here, and she could even make out a shoe print.

The CSIs would definitely need to process this.

"Do you smell that?" Aiden asked, and she snapped toward him to see where he was looking.

Not in the bathroom but the hall to their right. A hall that led back to the entrance of the building. And, yes, Lexa did smell something.

Smoke.

They barreled out of the bathroom, both of them racing toward the kitchen, only to realize the smoke wasn't coming from there but rather the front of the building. They went in that direction, skidding to a halt when she saw the front door was now shut. They had left it open. Lexa was certain of that.

"Gasoline," Aiden snarled.

Lexa smelled it, too. The strong, overpowering scent that seemed to coat every bit of the air in the room. It slammed together with the smoke seeping beneath and around the door.

And that's when Lexa saw something bad.

The blistering hot, red flames shooting against the windows.

--------- ☆ ---------

CHAPTER TWO

─────── ☆ ───────

Aiden cursed and caught onto Lexa. He latched onto her arm, dragging her away from that fire, from that window.

Not a second too soon.

The heat shattered the glass, sending a spray of shards all over the room. And right at them.

He pulled her behind one of the toppled chairs, both of them landing hard on the floor. They'd have bruises and scrapes. No doubt about that. But they'd have a whole lot more if they didn't get the hell out of there.

Because it wasn't just that one fire by that one window.

When Aiden glanced around, he could see that there were flames shooting up outside every single window. Someone was trying to burn them alive. Or cut them to ribbons because more glass shattered.

Lexa covered her head with one arm and gave the voice command for her phone to call 911. "This is Deputy Lexa Mullen. I need the fire department and police backup to the Yellow Rose

Manor now," she ordered.

Good. That was a start, but Aiden knew they couldn't stay here and wait the ten minutes or so it'd take the responders to get here.

"Let's move," Aiden insisted.

He still had hold of Lexa's arm, but she was already maneuvering herself off the floor. The moment they were both upright, they took off running in the direction of the kitchen toward what he hoped was an exit that hadn't been cut off with yet more flames.

Hell, why fire?

Was it a bad coincidence, or was some sonofabitch trying to recreate the nightmare where Lexa and he had nearly died. Where they'd both failed to save a hostage and nearly died in the process.

This isn't that fire, he mentally repeated to himself. *This isn't that nightmare.*

Fueled by the reminder—and the strong desire not to get their asses burned—Aiden sprinted toward the back of the building with Lexa right along beside him. They skidded to a stop in the kitchen.

And both cursed.

The thick black smoke was crawling around and underneath the door, and there were more of those flames outside the window. Someone had really been thorough in setting up this death trap.

He thought of the layout of the building. There were no windows in the restrooms, but the changing room had one so that's where they'd go. After they checked the other rooms to make sure no one else was trapped inside.

"This way," Aiden said, racing toward the men's room. Empty. And unlike the women's toilet, there was no blood in here.

They threw open the door of a storage room. Again, empty. No windows either, but the smoke was getting thicker, making it hard to breathe.

Lexa and he went to the office next, and Aiden kicked in the door. There was a window here.

And more fire outside it.

The glass had already broken, and the flames were licking their way into the room. Aiden shut the door and kept moving. Kept looking.

Along with having to fight the flashbacks, Aiden was also battling the frustration over basically having the crime scene shot to hell and back. This smoke, the spewing glass from the windows, and Lexa's and his own tracks were no doubt destroying potential evidence.

So, maybe this wasn't about Lexa and him.

Not about them being forced to relive their trek through hell.

Maybe it was about a killer or attacker making sure there had been nothing left behind that could be used to ID him or her.

Lexa started coughing when they had to run through a thick cloud of smoke, and they darted into the changing room, no doubt tracking over yet more critical evidence. His eyes and throat felt like sandpaper, and his lungs weren't fairing much better. Still, he could see well enough to realize there was no fire outside the small window.

"Keep watch," Aiden told Lexa.

Her eyes widened, and it probably occurred to her that the arsonist could be waiting outside. Maybe ready to gun them down. So, they might be damned if they stayed or damned if they went.

But they were going.

He could fight a gunman, but there was no fighting this fire that was creating a pressure cooker of smoke and scorching heat inside the building.

Aiden unlocked the window and tried to hoist it up. Emphasis on *tried*. But it jammed shut. That spiked up his heart rate some, but he went to that hyperfocus place that he'd created in his head for missions.

Work the problem. Survive. Rescue.

Because he wasn't having another repeat of what'd happened three years ago, when Lexa and he had ended up together battling a fire in a hostage situation. No. Wasn't having that.

"Close your eyes," Aiden told Lexa, and that was the only warning he gave her before he reared back and kicked the window.

Glass and bits of wood flew, but Aiden kept kicking, well aware this escape route was a double edge sword. Once the air was in the room, that would give the fire exactly what it wanted. Oxygen to feed and grow. And if there were flames already inside the building, they'd be racing like hell to get to their fuel.

Aiden gave the window another kick, and it finally gave way, enough of it falling so they could climb out. "I'll go out first and deal with anyone out there," he insisted. "You come out right behind me."

But Lexa didn't respond to that. She ran back to the center of the room and grabbed the dress. She wrapped it around him like protective gear before she shoved him out the window. There were still bits of broken glass clinging to what was left of the frame, and he could feel and hear them ripping away at the dress as he climbed through. That was good thinking on Lexa's part, and it saved him from needing stitches and losing some blood.

The moment his boots landed on the ground, Aiden did two things. He checked around them for a would be killer, and when he didn't spot anyone or anything other than smoke, he shoved the dress back into the opening, cocooning Lexa in it before he dragged her through the window.

Aiden didn't have to tell Lexa that they needed to run and take cover because like him, she hit the ground on the move. She tossed the dress away from the building, and she didn't just look around. Lexa also scoped out where they should run.

Her attention landed on the same spot Aiden's had seconds earlier. A fountain in a fancy-looking courtyard. No doubt a photo op spot for brides and grooms, but it was concrete and would provide a lot more protection than them being out in the open like this.

Lexa and he sprinted toward it, and with each step, Aiden braced himself for them to be shot at. That didn't happen. And when they finally were able to dive behind cover, they automatically pivoted, moving back to back so they could give themselves 360 degrees of surveillance.

And what he saw wasn't good.

No attacker, none that he could spot anyway. It was dark, going on nine pm, and there were wispy clouds covering the moon. But the fire was providing enough light for him to see the flames consuming the building. A whole hell of a lot of accelerant had been used to cause this much of an inferno this fast.

He felt the muscles in Lexa's back tense, and she shifted her gun toward some trees at the back of the property. Aiden shifted, too, looking in that direction, and he caught some movement. It was just a blink. Too fast for him to figure out if it was a person or just a moving tree branch.

Aiden considered rushing there to check it out, but that would mean darting right out in the open where he could be gunned down. Ditto for Lexa since she would almost certainly go with him. So, it was best to wait for backup and then they could search the grounds.

In the distance, he heard the wail of sirens, but Aiden tried to shut out the sound. Tried to tamp down his own heartbeat thundering in his ears. He had to listen. He had to be able to hear if anyone was moving in to ambush them.

Despite his best efforts, more of those flashbacks came. Images chopped and smeared together of smoke and blood. So much blood.

And the dead hostage.

He'd seen people die before. It came with the territory. But he'd never had someone die in his arms like she had.

Yeah, that wasn't going away *ever*.

Thankfully, the flashing blue lights cleared out the worst of the images. They were cutting through the darkness and smoke, too, and several moments later, an Outlaw Ridge PD cruiser sped into the driveway of the manor. He saw a welcome sight. His brother, Deputy Shaw Brodie, and the other swing shift deputy, Callie Brandon. That meant, they'd left his other brother, Declan, manning the office.

Shaw and Callie barreled out of the vehicle, not racing toward Lexa and him but rather taking cover behind the cruiser while they looked around.

"We're over here," Lexa called out. Aiden and she stayed behind cover as well.

"Is anyone in the building?" Shaw immediately wanted to know.

"I don't think so," Aiden replied. Of course, there could be a body stuffed somewhere inside, but the person who set the fires would have needed to be outside to do that.

"Are you hurt?" Callie asked.

"No," Lexa and he answered in unison. "But it's possible someone was killed inside," Aiden provided. "There's a hell of a lot of blood."

He heard Callie and his brother curse, but their voices were drowned out by the pulsing siren of the fire engine. It roared to a stop, and those responders sprang into action.

Since Aiden figured an attacker would now be on the run, he stood, still staying vigilant. Lexa did as well, and she gathered the wedding dress into as much of a ball as she could. Esther had been right about the poofy part. But the woman had been wrong about vandals causing the damage.

No, they were looking at something much worse than vandalism.

And the person who'd bled all over the Yellow Rose Manor could be out here somewhere.

That reminder got Aiden moving. "Fan out," he called out to Shaw and Callie.

No need for him to explain what they should be looking for. Like Lexa, Callie was a veteran cop with more than a decade of experience. Shaw had been an Air Force Combat Rescue Officer and was currently a Strike Force operative and temporary deputy. They'd be on the lookout for anything and everything.

When Lexa headed toward the south end of the property, Aiden took the north, and he went to the right of the driveway where there was some fancy rose garden setup. He'd only gone a few yards when he spotted something.

Two large gasoline cans.

Judging from the way they were laying on their sides, they were empty.

Aiden used the flashlight on his phone to examine the area around the cans, and he thought he spotted a shoeprint. Unlike the bloody one in the bathroom, CSI would be able to examine this one.

He looked up when there was a slash of headlights. Not the CSIs though as he'd hoped. But he recognized the blue truck. And the driver.

Brady Kern.

The soon-to-be groom.

"Shit," Aiden growled, and he started toward their visitor. What was he doing here?

Brady threw open his truck door, practically falling out. His eyes were wide and fixed on the blaze that was still going strong. "Chloe," he shouted, and he started a mad dash toward the manor.

Aiden cursed again and took off running so he could intercept him. The activity must have gotten Lexa's attention, too, because she tossed down the gown and sprinted in their direction.

"Chloe!" Brady yelled.

Aiden hooked his arms around the man, holding him in place. He outsized Brady by a good thirty pounds, but adrenaline was a big factor here, and his former SEAL pal was fighting like a wildcat to get loose. Aiden couldn't blame him. If he believed someone he loved was in that building, nothing would have stopped him from rushing inside.

And probably getting killed in the process.

Both Brady and he had plenty of training, but the firemen were the experts here, not them. They'd just get in the way. It was impossible for that to get through to Brady though, and the man kept trying to push off Aiden's hold.

Lexa moved in to help, and the three of them ended up in a wrestling match that landed them on the ground. During all of the fray, Brady didn't take his eyes off the manor.

"Chloe," he repeated, but this time it wasn't a shout. It was a hoarse sob that tore from his throat. "She's in there. Chloe's in there."

"Lexa and I didn't see her, but if she's there, the firemen will look for her," Aiden assured him, and he checked over his shoulder to verify that some of the firemen were indeed going in. They were. "Why did you come here?" he tacked onto that.

For a moment or two it didn't seem as if Brady had heard the question, but he finally muttered, "Esther Drummond. She called me and told me there'd been trouble at the manor."

Hell in a big assed handbasket. He wished Esther hadn't done that, but then word would have quickly gotten around anyway. Gossip could travel faster than the speed of light in a small town.

"Are you sure Chloe came here?" Lexa asked.

Brady nodded, along with making another of those sobs. He still didn't take his eyes off the building.

"Chloe's car isn't here," Lexa pointed out.

Another nod from Brady. "She told me yesterday she was coming, that she'd already dropped off her dress, and that she'd walk from her place."

Aiden had to thumb through his memory to recall where Chloe lived. On Third Street, not far from the high school, and the manor was all the way at the edge of town, at the end of a road. Not exactly right around the block from her. It was more like a half of a mile.

"Chloe was going to try on her shoes and practice coming down the aisle," Brady explained. "They're a higher heel than she usually wears, and she didn't want to trip."

"Other than you, who knew that Chloe would be coming here tonight?" Lexa pressed.

Brady finally tore his gaze from the fire and looked at her. His forehead bunched up. "I, uh, don't know. Why?"

Lexa and Aiden exchanged a glance, and even though they didn't say anything to each other, he understood what she was thinking. She didn't want to mention all that blood, but Brady's attention slid in the direction of the wedding gown that Lexa had tossed on the ground.

"Is that Chloe's dress?" he asked, even more alarm creeping into his eyes.

Lexa didn't get a chance to answer because Shaw called out, "Aiden, Lexa, back here."

There was plenty of urgency and concern in his brother's voice, and Aiden and Lexa got to their feet. "Stay here," Lexa told Brady. "And that's an order. Let the firemen do their jobs and stay out of their way."

That might work, but Aiden continued to fire some glances over his shoulder at Brady as Lexa and he made their way toward the far back left of the building. There were no flames here, just a small semicircle of yard rimmed with massive oaks. Shaw and Callie were standing next to one of those trees, and they had their attention staked to the ground.

"What is it?" Lexa asked, hurrying to them.

"Blood and drag marks," Shaw provided. He pointed to something. "And that."

Callie had her phone flashlight aimed at a spot where the grass ended and the mulch around the tree began. On top of that mulch, the flashlight glinted on something.

Hell.

It was an engagement ring. A familiar one. And the last time Aiden had seen it, it'd been on Chloe's finger.

───── ☆ ─────

CHAPTER THREE

———— ☆ ————

Lexa wasn't the least bit surprised when Aiden and she stepped into the police station, and she saw the sheriff waiting for them in the deputies' bullpen. In the nearly four months that she'd worked for Owen, she had found him to be a very involved boss.

A possible dead body, the fire, and Aiden's and her brush with death would be more than enough to have him show up.

"Are you both all right?" Owen immediately asked.

Aiden nodded, and she muttered, "Yes."

Though they probably didn't look all right. Their clothes reeked of smoke and were charred in spots where embers had landed on them. Her shirt also had blood on it, no doubt from where she'd wrapped the wedding dress around her. But other than their rough appearance, Aiden and she had fared well. They were alive, and her only injuries were a few scrapes and bruises.

Owen made a sound as if he was assessing their responses. Assessing them, too, and he didn't quite seem to buy that "all right" insistences. Still, he didn't call them on it, but instead shifted his attention to Brady, who had ridden there in the cruiser with them. Callie and Shaw were standing behind the man.

"Brady," Owen greeted. Since Owen had been raised in Outlaw Ridge, he not only knew Brady, but rumor had it that he'd also once dated Brady's late mother when they'd been teenagers.

Small worlds often complicated the devil out of situations like this. Objectivity could be a hard fought battle. But Owen was no doubt well aware that in cases of murdered women, the spouse or partner was usually the most likely suspect.

And Brady was indeed just that.

Because of that small world thing, Lexa hoped that Brady hadn't offed his fiancée because if he had, that meant he had also likely been responsible for Aiden and her coming close to being burned alive.

Yeah, she didn't want Brady to have done any of that.

"Callie, could you please take Brady to interview room one?" Owen asked. "Get him some water or a soda, and if he wants, let him call his lawyer."

Brady made a strangled sound, a mix of a huff and a gasp. "My lawyer? Why would I need…"

His words trailed off, and realization must have sunk in. He didn't get angry or shout out that he was innocent. Maybe because there was a hefty amount of shock playing into this. Brady lowered his head, and there was zero trace of the fearless Navy SEAL that he'd once been as he followed Callie out of the bullpen.

Owen watched them leave, and he didn't say anything else until Brady was out of earshot. "I've already taken Esther's statement and then let her go. She didn't tell me anything that I think we can use to solve this case. It's the same for the buttload of calls from people who saw the fire department and other responders but no actual attack or arsonist."

"I'm guessing one of those calls didn't come from Chloe herself," Lexa muttered, hoping but knowing that was a serious long shot.

"No, I had Hayes and Jemma go to Chloe's place, but she wasn't there," Owen explained, referring to the two deputies. Since the pair wasn't on swing shift, Owen had obviously called them in. "Her doors were all locked, and the place looked secured. From what they could see through the windows, there were no signs of a struggle. Since there was some question about Chloe's whereabouts and possible safety, they jimmied the lock and went inside. No Chloe."

So, that ruled out the possibility that the woman was at home and had merely left her things at the manor before...well, whatever the hell was that had happened.

"According to Brady, Chloe was going to walk from her place to the manor so her car wasn't there," Aiden let Owen know.

Owen nodded. "It's parked in front of Chloe's house. The CSIs will go over it just in case there's anything to find."

Lexa doubted there would be since it hadn't been near the site of all that blood. Still, examining her vehicle and her house were investigative boxes that had to be checked off.

"Did you manage to get in touch with Lily Whitaker?" Lexa asked. Because that was another box that needed checking off. The owner of the manor might give them some critical info.

"I did," Owen verified. "She said that Chloe mentioned wanting to come to the manor, but there were no firm plans. Chloe did have a key to the place," he added before Lexa could ask. "Apparently, she picked it up a few days ago when she brought over the dress."

So, a key but no set time for Chloe to be at the manor. That didn't exactly conflict with what Brady had said. But it didn't verify his account either.

Owen stared at them. "What I want to know is, has there actually been a murder, and second, did Brady do it?"

Aiden and Lexa exchanged a glance. And a sigh. "We didn't find a body," Aiden spelled out. "What we did find was a whole lot of blood in both the changing room and the women's restroom. There were also some drops and smears in the hall leading between those two rooms."

"Enough blood to indicate Chloe could be dead?" Owen asked.

Lexa shook her head, then shrugged. "Not sure. Like Aiden said, there was a lot of it, but it was mainly spatters, drops, and castoff except for one puddle in the dressing room."

Owen took a moment, obviously processing that. "So, maybe a body or someone with serious injuries. And maybe it's Chloe."

"Her purse was in the changing room, and her phone was in the bathroom," Lexa pointed out. "And Brady said that she had gone to the manor to practice walking down the aisle." She pulled in a breath and hated that she also dragged in the stench of that smoke and blood. "There was also some damage in the main room where the ceremonies and receptions are held. Broken vases, trampled flowers, overturned chairs. That could have been from a struggle."

It didn't take a vivid imagination to see how it could have played out. Someone could have walked in on Chloe while she was at the manor. Chloe could have tried to get away and was stabbed, shot or hit with a blunt object in the process.

"There were drag marks and more blood behind the manor," Shaw added, taking up the explanation. "That's where we found the ring. The CSIs and Declan are there now combing through the area. There's something else you need to know," Shaw tacked onto that before Owen could respond. "Night before last, Brady and Chloe had one hell of an argument at Outlaw's Rest."

Owen, Aiden, and Lexa all turned in Shaw's direction. The Outlaw's Rest was an old-timey saloon on the edge of town, and while Lexa didn't go there very often, she knew it was a popular place.

"I was there," Shaw went on, "and I don't know what started the argument, but it got pretty intense. They kept their voices muffled, but then Chloe threw a drink in Brady's face and stormed out."

Lexa groaned. Damn it. That didn't make things look good for Brady.

Owen obviously felt the same. "Shit," he snarled, and he scrubbed his hand over his face. "I'm guessing Chloe didn't call off the wedding if according to Brady, she'd gone to the manor to practice her walk."

The silence settled over them for a couple of snail-crawling moments. And Lexa figured they were all thinking the same thing.

That they couldn't take Brady at his word.

In fact, it was possible that maybe Chloe had ended things with him. Then, if she'd gone to manor to get her dress, Brady could have followed her and killed her there.

"All right," Owen said, shifting his attention back to Shaw. "Find me anything you can on the argument that the *lovebirds* had at Outlaw's Rest. I'm sure there'll be plenty who have their own version of events. Then, see if anyone knows about

Chloe calling off the wedding."

"Will do," Shaw assured him, already taking out his phone and heading to his desk.

"I need photos of the ring and the wedding dress to show Brady," Owen said, turning back toward Aiden and her.

Aiden held up his phone. "I snapped them right before we left the manor. The CSIs took both items for processing."

Lexa had watched the CSIs bag the items and label them as top priority. The dress was ripped and sooty, but that big blood stain still showed up loud and clear. And since both Aiden's and her DNA and prints were on file, the lab would be able to rule out any trace they'd left behind.

Owen slid glances at both Aiden and her. "Are you two up to being in the interview with Brady?"

"Yes," she couldn't answer fast enough. Lexa wanted to know what the man had to say. Aiden obviously felt the same since he gave a quick nod.

Owen motioned for them to follow him, and they made their way down the hall with its freshly painted walls and new tiled flooring. That *newness* applied to the entire building that Owen had personally paid to have renovated after it'd been damaged when most of the police force had been killed.

It was impossible for Lexa to walk this hall and not remember that.

But the newness also made her made her think of fresh starts. And she had to pray that nothing like that would ever happen again, especially with all the security equipment Owen had had installed. No killer would be able to just walk in and start murdering cops.

Owen, Aiden, and she stepped into the interview room to find Callie by the door and Brady pacing like a caged tiger. The gravity of the situation had clearly sunk in, and Brady was no longer in the stage of hanging his head. Nope. There was fire in his pale blue eyes.

Because of that no degrees of separation, Lexa forced herself to look at Brady as if she'd never seen him before. He was tall and lanky with blond hair and a light complexion. He was basically a reverse image of Aiden's features of black hair and brown eyes.

There was no blood on Brady's clothes, and Lexa couldn't see any scratches or bruises anywhere on him. That was in no way conclusive proof that he hadn't been in some kind of altercation. It was possible that Chloe simply hadn't been able to fight back.

"I need you to help Shaw with what he's working on," Owen told Callie. "And try to chase down any preliminary reports from the CSIs."

"I didn't do anything to harm Chloe," Brady insisted as Callie exited the room.

Owen held up his hand in a wait a second gesture, and he gave a verbal command to turn on the recorder. Once he named the date, time, and everyone present, they all sat at the table, and he recited the Miranda warning to Brady.

Brady squeezed his eyes shut and groaned. "I didn't kill her," he insisted when Owen had finished. "I love Chloe. We're getting married the day after tomorrow."

Owen didn't respond to any of that. "Deputy Brodie, could you please show Brady the photos."

Aiden complied, lifting his phone so that Brady could see the pictures. "Do you recognize either of these things?" he asked.

Brady's mouth went tight. "Yes, that's Chloe's engagement ring, and I think that's her wedding dress. What happened to it?" he quickly tacked onto that. "What happened to her?"

"That's what we're trying to find out," Owen assured him.

"There's blood on the dress," Brady muttered, and he swallowed hard. "Is it Chloe's? Has she been hurt?"

Owen lifted his shoulder. "We don't know yet. The dress is on the way to the lab. If Chloe's DNA isn't in the database, then the CSIs will try to get a sample from her house to try to use as a match. Or they can maybe get it from a close relative."

"Her brother, Hudson," Brady volunteered. "He's a bartender and lives in San Antonio." He took out his phone and showed them the number in his contacts. "Their parents are dead, so it's just the two of them."

"I don't recall ever seeing Hudson around," Lexa said, jotting down the number on the notepad that was already on the table.

"No," Brady agreed. Another pause, and the muscles stirred in his jaw. "Hudson and I don't get along. He, uh, didn't want Chloe to marry me."

Interesting. And it gave them another person of interest in this possible murder. At Owen's nod, Lexa texted Callie so she could get started on locating Chloe's brother.

"Brady, when's the last time you saw your fiancée?" Owen asked.

He glanced at the clock. "About five hours ago. I was at my office, finishing up some work, and she dropped by to see me and to tell me about her plans to go to the manor."

Lexa made a note of that, too. Brady was a lawyer in his dad's firm, and the building was right next to the town's pharmacy. That meant there'd be security cameras that might have recorded Chloe's visit.

"Your wedding is supposed to be in two days, and you were working," Owen pointed out. "No stag party? No last minute things to deal with?"

"The party was last weekend," Brady said, and he got a confirming sound of agreement from Aiden. "And as for the wedding details, Chloe wanted to handle all of that. She insisted the only thing I had to do was show up."

That meshed with what Lexa knew about the woman. Chloe was a CPA, and if the gossip was true, she liked to be in charge.

"Why did Chloe visit you at your office?" Owen

continued a moment later.

Some color flushed on the man's cheeks. "To do some more kissing and making up. We'd had a spat the night before last. We resolved that," Brady was quick to add. "But Chloe wanted to make sure there were no hard feelings left between us."

"And was there?" Lexa asked.

"No," Brady snapped. "We had worked all of that out."

"What exactly did you have to work out?" Aiden asked. "What was the argument about?"

Brady opened his mouth, closed it, and then shook his head. "Chloe was upset because she'd heard talk about me kissing a stripper at my bachelor's party. I hadn't. But she was mad, and I didn't handle it right. I tried to joke about it, and she, well, she threw her drink at me. She's never done anything like that before."

Lexa had certainly never heard of that happening, and in a small town, that kind of juicy gossip wouldn't have stayed secret. "I take it Chloe is the jealous type?" she wanted to know.

Brady shook his head, shrugged. "She never has been, but I guess that hit a nerve with her. Plus, she's super stressed about the wedding, so I think she overreacted. But we made up," he emphasized.

Again, that would be something they'd have to check. Someone would likely recall seeing Brady and Chloe in public since that argument at the saloon.

"Where were you this evening before you

showed up at the Yellow Rose Manor?" Owen asked.

"Home," Brady answered without hesitation, but judging from his expression, he seemed to think that was a trick question. "I, uh, left work shortly after Chloe dropped by, went home, ate dinner, and showered. Chole had said she might drop by after she did the walking rehearsal."

"Showered," Owen repeated, and Lexa heard the concern in her boss' tone. It was possible that Brady was telling the truth about his evening. But the shower could have been taken to wash away any blood from an attack.

"Chloe and you don't live together?" Owen asked, though he no doubt already knew the answer.

"No. Chloe's old-fashioned like that. She didn't want us to live as a couple until we were married."

"Will you consent to us searching your house?" Owen pressed. "Or do we need to get a warrant?"

"Search it." Again, Brady was quick with that. "Do whatever you need to do to try to find Chloe." He stopped and glanced at his phone. "Hell. I need to call my dad. I don't want him to hear about this through the gossip mill."

Lexa was surprised Brady's father, Wylie, hadn't already heard. And hadn't already called. Chloe wasn't the only person in town with a reputation for wanting to control things. That description fit Wylie to a tee.

"My dad thought Chloe would call off the

wedding," Brady said under her breath.

"Why is that?" Owen didn't waste any time asking.

Brady flushed again. "Because he thought Chloe was after family money. She wasn't," he snapped out. And there was obviously some anger about his father's opinion. "Chloe loves me, and I love her."

The words had barely left his mouth when a shout rang out. "I will see the sonofabitch now," someone yelled.

Brady got to his feet. "That's Chloe's brother, Hudson. He might know where Chloe is."

With that, Brady rushed to the door, and Owen didn't stop him. He merely said, for the sake of the recording, "Interview paused. All parties exiting the room." And he added the time before they hurried out after Brady.

"Let me see him," Hudson yelled, his voice seemingly echoing through the whole building.

They rushed into the bullpen area to find Shaw trying to restrain the beefy brown-haired man. Lexa noted the family resemblance. Noted, too, that Hudson was about to burst with fury.

Fury that he aimed at Brady when his narrowed gaze landed on him.

"There you are, you sonofabitch," Hudson snarled. He took a swing at Shaw, clearly trying to break free of him.

Hudson rammed his elbow into Shaw's gut, and both Owen and Aiden hurried forward to help control the man. Hudson had to be fueled by a whopping amount of rage and adrenaline because he tried to fight all three.

A fight he soon lost.

Aiden outmuscled the larger man, pinning his arms in place while Shaw cuffed him. "Put him in a cell until he calms down," Owen insisted.

"I'm not calming down," Hudson snarled, tacking on some vicious profanity. Again, that was all aimed at Brady, who was stock still at the back of the room. "Not until you arrest that sonofabitch."

"Arrest him for what?" Lexa demanded.

Hudson didn't take his attention off Brady. "For murdering my sister. He killed her. I know he did."

─────── ☆ ───────

CHAPTER FOUR

———— ☆ ————

Aiden had to tighten his grip on Hudson when he tried to go after Brady again. This night had already been a pisser, but apparently, it was about to get worse. Well, worse if Brady had truly murdered Chloe.

Right now, Aiden didn't intend to take the word of Chloe's cursing, spoiling for a fight brother.

"Lock him up," Owen snarled when Hudson tried to kick him.

Shaw took hold of Hudson's right arm. Aiden, his left. And while the man continued to spew accusations and generally make himself a pain in the ass, Shaw and he perp walked Hudson to the middle hall that contained the cells. Thanks to the upgrades Owen had made, the cells no longer had bars but thick safety glass with a metal flap door for delivering meals and such.

It took some doing to get the man inside the enclosure because Hudson was as strong as an ox. A really pissed-off one. But Shaw and Aiden finally got his butt locked up.

The battle wasn't over yet though since they had to search Hudson for potential weapons. He'd made it through the metal detector at the front of the station without setting it off so he likely didn't have a gun or a knife.

And he didn't, Aiden discovered during the pat down.

No shoelaces or other objects either that could be used for self-harm. However, Aiden took his cell phone and keys before Shaw and he stepped out, shut the door, and then Aiden gave Hudson the Miranda warning.

"Put your hands through the opening so I can take off the cuffs," Shaw instructed. Hudson did after the man spewed out more profanity, and Shaw used his pocketknife to snip the plastic.

"Lawyer," Hudson shouted as they walked away. "And then I can sue you for being fucking idiots. You should be locking up Brady, not me."

"And you shouldn't be assaulting the cops," Aiden shot right back at him. Though even after four months, it still didn't feel right to call himself a cop since it was a temporary position. Nevertheless, he had the badge for now, and he wanted to help.

Correction: he needed to help.

If a woman had truly been murdered and his old friend was responsible, then some hard justice needed to be served. Aiden would help Owen do that in any way he could. In more ways than one, Owen had saved him, and he wouldn't forget that.

"You okay?" Shaw asked as they made their way back to the bullpen.

"Been better," Aiden admitted.

Shaw made a sound of agreement. "If you need me to switch off partners and work with Lexa, just let me know."

His brother was well aware of the shitstorm ordeal that'd happened when Lexa and he had failed to save a hostage. To save Mandie. And, yeah, sometimes being around Lexa triggered godawful flashbacks. But being around her stirred other things, too. A reminder that there'd been instant heat between them. A lust at first sight kind of deal. And despite the trigger junk, that heat apparently wasn't going away.

"I'll work with her," Aiden told his brother.

In fact, he wanted to work with her. Hell, wanted to be with her. So, that meant the flashbacks and other crap were just going to have to deal with that.

When they returned to the bullpen, Aiden saw that Brady and Callie were no longer there. Callie had likely ushered him back to the interview room. But Lexa and Owen were still around, and they were studying something on the laptop screen on her desk.

"Hudson's clamoring about a lawyer," Shaw relayed to Owen.

"Let him make a call," Owen said, keeping his attention on the computer.

Lexa looked up, her gaze connecting with

Aiden's. Yeah, that heat wasn't going anywhere. But there was plenty of concern in her dark blue eyes.

"We just got Chloe's phone records," she let him know.

That got Aiden moving closer while Shaw headed back in the direction of the cell, no doubt to help Hudson contact a lawyer.

"The last call that Chloe got was from Brady four hours ago," Owen pointed out.

Yep, Aiden saw that. Also saw that the call had only lasted nine seconds. Likely too long for it to have been a butt dial or such, but that wasn't a lot of time for an actual conversation.

He thought of the argument Brady and Chloe had had at the bar. Thought about her throwing the drink in his face and then storming out. Brady had insisted they'd kissed and made up, but he wasn't seeing anything in her phone records to indicate that.

"This was the only time Brady had called her since the incident at Outlaw's Rest," Aiden commented. "But I count eleven calls and multiple texts during that time to her brother."

Both Lexa and Owen made sounds of agreement. "We should be getting transcripts of the texts soon," Owen said.

Good. Because he very much wanted to know what the siblings had discussed. They could maybe get that from Hudson's phone but for any actual conversations, they'd have to rely on Hudson himself for that info.

"Chloe made and got a handful of calls to the owner of the manor," Lexa muttered, going down the list as well. "Several to the florist…" She stopped when she came to a name that she obviously recognized.

So did Aiden.

Wylie Kern, Brady's father.

Aiden supposed it wasn't a huge surprise that Wylie might want to talk to his soon-to-be daughter-in-law, but this is where rumors played into things. There was plenty of gossip about Wylie not approving of the marriage because Brady and Chloe had only been involved for about six months. And Brady had said that his dad believed Chloe was essentially a gold digger.

"Keep checking the list," Owen instructed, taking out his phone and stepping to the side. "I'll give Wylie a call." The man must have answered because it wasn't long before Owen said, "Hello, Wylie."

"I figured as close as Brady and his father are that he would have already been here," Aiden muttered.

"Yes," Lexa was quick to agree. "Maybe he's out of town or already in bed."

True. Because if he'd been home and awake, he likely would have heard about the fire and Brady's *detainment* despite living on his palatial ranch that was several miles outside of town.

"Wylie's already on his way and will be here

in a couple of minutes," Owen relayed when he finished the call. He was about to say something else, but his phone rang. "Clay Sanchez," he let them know.

The owner of Outlaw's Rest. Maybe he could shed some light on the argument that Chloe and Brady had had. Again, Owen stepped to the side to take the call, and Lexa and Aiden continued with the phone records.

"What seems to be missing are calls to friends back in San Antonio where Chloe was born and raised," Aiden pointed out.

She scanned through the list again. "You're right. With the exception of her brother, these are all local calls."

They were, and excluding those to Hudson, Wylie, and Brady, most were connected to wedding planning. A few other names he recognized as likely clients for the CPA work that Chloe did.

"Maybe Chloe didn't have a lot of friends," Lexa remarked, but he could tell from her tone that her interest had been piqued. "Did Brady ever say why she'd moved to Outlaw Ridge?"

He had to thumb back through the handful of conversations he'd had with Brady over the past six months since Chloe had moved to town.

"Yeah. Apparently, Brady and she met at a party in San Antonio and hit it off. They started dating, and she moved here to be closer to him. He asked her to marry him shortly afterward."

Aiden was still giving that some thought when Owen finished his call. "Argument confirmed between Chloe and Brady," he announced. "Clay said it got loud and intense, but the only part of it he heard for sure was that Chloe thought Brady had cheated on her at the bachelor's party. Were you at the party?" he asked Aiden.

Aiden nodded. "Briefly. I was wiped after a long shift and only stayed about an hour. And, yes, there were strippers. I didn't see Brady kiss one of them, but it's possible."

He glanced at Lexa who seemed to be doing her damnest not to look at him. Was she wondering if he'd done any stripper kissing? Or maybe that was wishful thinking on his part that she might be a smidge jealous that something like that could have happened.

The front door opened, causing the three of them to shift in that direction, and even though Aiden had expected it to be Wylie, it wasn't. However, it was someone he knew, Gillian Petty, the office assistant who worked for Wylie and Brady at their law firm.

"I just heard," Gillian blurted as she raced in. She was pale, trembling, and her eyes were red, maybe from crying. "Is Brady all right? Was he hurt in the fire?"

"Brady wasn't hurt," Owen assured her.

The woman let out a long breath and pressed her hand to the front of her workout tank. "Thank God. I was so worried about him when I heard there'd been a fire at the manor."

Aiden frowned. She'd been worried about Brady but not Chloe? Interesting, but it meshed with what he knew about Gillian. According to Brady and the gossip he'd heard, Gillian had had a thing for Brady that had been going on since elementary school. As far as Aiden was aware, Brady hadn't returned those feelings one bit.

"Can I see Brady?" Gillian asked. "Where is he?" There was more than an edge of desperation to her tone and expression.

Owen shook his head. "Sorry, but we need to talk with Brady first. Why don't you give him a call in the morning?"

Obviously, that wasn't what Gillian wanted to hear. Her shoulders dropped. Tears filled her eyes. But she nodded. "All right. Uh, please tell him I was here and that I'd been worried about him. If he needs anything, all he has to do is let me know."

Gillian turned to leave, but Owen stopped her with a question. "When's the last time you saw Chloe?"

The woman blinked. "Chloe?" she repeated as if the question was a surprise. She shook her head. "I'm not sure. A couple of weeks ago maybe when she dropped by to see Brady. Why?"

"Just gathering info," Owen replied. "What about earlier today? Did Chloe come by the law office?"

Gillian opened her mouth. Closed it. And seemed to rethink what she'd been about to say.

"I'm not sure. I was in and out all day. Errands and such. Why? She repeated.

Owen did a repeat, too. "Just gathering info. You can go now, and if I have more questions for you, I'll let you know."

Gillian stared at him a moment later, seemingly trying to suss out if there was a hidden meaning in that, and she finally walked out.

Just as Wylie came rushing in.

He muttered something to Gillian that Aiden didn't catch and left her in the doorway as he came closer to Owen, Lexa, and him. Gillian gave them all one last look before she finally left.

"Where's Brady? Is he all right?" Wylie asked, echoing what Gillian had demanded when she'd come in.

Aiden knew that father and son were close, along with being a spitting image of each other. It was as if Wylie was a twenty-year older version of Brady himself.

"He's fine," Owen assured him. "He's in the interview room."

"Is he under arrest?" Wylie blurted.

"No." But Owen's tone seemed to add *for now*. "I need to finish taking his statement, and then you can see him."

Wylie huffed out a breath that was a mix of relief and more of that worry. "Esther called me and said Chloe might be dead."

Good grief. Esther could sure blab. Funny though that that bit about Chloe hadn't made it to Gillian's ears. But then, maybe it had, and Gillian hadn't cared what had happened to Brady's fiancée.

"We don't know Chloe's status right now," Owen explained. "That's what we're trying to find out." He paused. "Were you aware of any trouble between Brady and her?"

"You mean that argument at the bar," Wylie was quick to say. "Yeah, I knew about that." He shook his head and squeezed his eyes shut for a moment. "Brady should have never gotten involved with her. She's bad news."

Aiden looked at Owen and Lexa to see if that surprised them. It didn't. Which meant they'd no doubt heard the gossip, too.

"Bad news how?" Owen pressed.

"Well, for one thing, I've caught her in a lie. I ran into her in San Antonio when I was there on business, and she'd told Brady she had to work all day here at her office in Outlaw Ridge. She was having lunch with her brother, and they seemed to be having a tense conversation until they spotted me."

Owen shrugged. "Maybe the lunch wasn't planned. So, not really a lie, just something that happened last minute."

"Maybe, but I got the gut feeling she just hadn't been truthful with Brady about that. And there's more. She doesn't look at Brady as if she's in love with him. I've caught her practically glaring at him a time or two."

"I'm in a relationship, and I can tell you that couples glare at each other every now and then," Owen admitted.

Wylie huffed and tapped his stomach. "Gut feel. Something is way off with Chloe, and whatever happened tonight at the manor, she could have set it up to make Brady look guilty of something."

That caused a silence to settle over the room, and it wasn't as if they could totally dismiss what Wylie had just said. The bottom line was that none of them knew Chloe that well.

"Why did you call Chloe three days ago?" Aiden asked.

For just a second, a flash of panic sprinted across the man's face, but it was gone as fast as it'd come. "I needed to find out what time I was supposed to be at the manor and if there was anything she needed me to do before then."

Hell. The man was lying. And he wasn't very good at it, either.

Owen would have no doubt pressed Wylie on that if Shaw had come walking in. He glanced at Wylie, then at the rest of them. "I need a word," he said, tipping his head to Owen, Lexa, and Aiden.

The three left Wylie and went to the back of the bullpen, and Shaw immediately handed Owen a phone. "It's Hudson's, and he wants us to look at the last text his sister sent him. A text she sent about five hours ago."

With plenty of concern on his face, Owen took

the phone, holding the screen so that Lexa and Aiden could read it. Aiden did.

And he cursed when the words practically jumped right at him.

I'm so scared, Chloe had texted. *I think I've made a bad mistake. I think he might try to kill me.*

———— ☆ ————

CHAPTER FIVE

Lexa rarely slept well during the middle of an investigation, and this particular one had been no exception. Especially since this case involved her working alongside Aiden.

She'd dreamed. *The* nightmare again. A tangled mix of real images and others that hadn't actually happened. Like Aiden and her dying at the hands of the young woman they'd failed to save, followed by all three of them being consumed by fire. It had taken a long shower and several cups of coffee to push those images aside and deal with the current ones.

Of that blood on the wedding dress.

And the text Chloe had sent her brother.

I'm so scared. I think I've made a bad mistake. I think he might try to kill me.

Yes, all of that was going to take some dealing with, and there'd be multiple steps in trying to get to the truth. Step one was to pay another visit to the crime scene and look at it in the morning light with the hopes of seeing something, anything, that she'd missed the night before.

After that, she'd show up way early for her shift and go through any updates or reports. She already knew that Owen had sent Brady home, rescheduling the rest of his interview for ten o'clock this morning. That'd been a solid move on Owen's part to give them time to build a case against Brady.

If there was a case to build, that is.

Chloe hadn't specifically mentioned Brady's name in the text to Hudson, and the woman could have been talking about someone else. That's where some hard digging and police work came into play. They'd need to identify every possible candidate for that "he" who'd frightened Chloe.

Lexa figured by now Owen had gotten a start on that list. Also, that her boss would have a much clearer picture of things. A better picture anyway than he had when Aiden and she had finally called it a day. That'd been shortly after two AM, and they'd left to their respective homes. Hers, here in town, and his somewhere on the outskirts of Outlaw Ridge.

After some of that broken sleep, she'd woken up to a text from Owen with a series of updates. Hudson had made bail and would be coming back in as well for an interview. Wylie would be, too. And the search for Chloe was still ongoing but with no results.

It was as if the woman had simply vanished.

But had she been murdered or was she injured somewhere? No way to know that unless they got a break in the investigation.

Lexa filled her thermos with coffee and drove the short distance to the manor. Of course, everything was a short distance in a small town, and it would only take her a couple of minutes to get there. She hoped no one else would be around so she could have some thinking time.

But solo clearly wasn't in the cards.

When she pulled into the parking lot, she spotted the CSI van, the fire chief's truck. And Aiden. He was standing there looking like a modern-day warrior eyeing a battlefield.

A modern-day *hot* warrior.

She sighed, not bothering to curse her body's reaction to him. But his class A looks did solve one problem for her. The remnants of the nightmare vanished in a blink.

Leave it to Aiden to perform a little miracle like that just by existing.

He turned toward her, and even the morning sun adored him since it seemed to frame his amazing body. Six-three. All lean muscle. All primed and ready for whatever might get tossed at him.

The corner of his mouth lifted in a quick, near smile. "Like minds," he muttered. "I wanted to get a look at the place."

"Like minds," she agreed, stepping to his side to study it.

Despite its label of a *manor*, it was more like a scaled-down version of Tara in *Gone with the Wind*.

One story with large columns on the porch that stretched across the entire front. Most of the wood was no longer white but rather streaked with the damage from the fire and smoke. Still, the building was standing, more or less, thanks to the quick response from the fire department.

Lexa glanced at the window where Aiden and she had escaped and got hit with the memory of that frantic rush to get the hell out of there. Not an easy thing to shrug off, but she managed it.

"Have they found anything else?" Lexa asked, tipping her head to the pair of CSIs who were by the trees. Dustin Caldwell and Emily Brooks, both friends from high school, and Lexa knew they were good at their jobs.

"No. They're examining those possible drag marks," Aiden explained. "The fire chief and an arson investigator are inside checking things out there. Once they give the okay, the CSIs will go in and see what they can find. It could be hours before we know anything."

So, Aiden had gotten some good info, and it made her wonder how long he'd been there. Apparently, her early start to the day hadn't been especially early after all.

"Did you see the report from the lab about the blood?" he asked.

She nodded. It wasn't good news. "Chloe's DNA isn't in the system."

And that meant the techs would have to extract several samples of DNA from items that had belonged to Chloe, along with getting a sample from her brother. All of that took time, and it was time when they wouldn't know for certain if the blood in the manor even belonged to Chloe.

"After talking with Owen, I also started a deep dive on both Chloe and Hudson," Aiden continued a moment later. "It's what Owen calls the whole shebang. Social media, any and all mentions on the internet, and public records. Strike Force has a decent database for that so I plugged in the info, and when I have some hits, we can go through them if you like."

"Definitely," she couldn't say fast enough. And she hesitated before voicing one of the things that had been on her mind. "Since you've had some thinking time, do you think Brady could have killed Chloe and done all of this?" She motioned to the fire damage on the manor.

Aiden hardly moved a muscle, but he still managed to convey a whole lot of emotions. The quick flash of dread that went through his eyes, darkening them even more than they already were. The slight tensing of his mouth. The barely-there exhale of breath.

"I don't want to believe it," he finally admitted. "And, yeah, going textbook, that could make me a liability in this investigation. But I swear I won't let my friendship with Brady dick around with what needs to be done."

She believed him and felt the same way. "I'm friends with Brady, too. Heck, every deputy on the force is, but if he killed Chloe, that won't stop any one of us from arresting him."

Lexa just hoped he hadn't ended his fiancée's life or been responsible for that blood they found in the manor. Still, there weren't a lot of other suspects. Not yet anyway. And that's where Aiden's whole shebang deep dive might help.

"I'm breaking a confidence by telling you this," Aiden added a moment later, "but Brady's dealing with PTSD from some things that happened when he was on active duty."

Considering Aiden and Brady had been on several deployments to classified locations, that was understandable. "How does his PTSD manifest itself?" Lexa asked.

"Nothing I've personally witnessed, but he admitted that sometimes the flashbacks get so bad that he has to take prescription meds."

That didn't sound good, and it was going to be hard to access any info from his medical records. Maybe though Brady would spill all, and if he was truly innocent, there'd be no reason for him not to do that.

"Do you have PTSD?" she asked.

He glanced away, shook his head. "Not too much."

The answer puzzled her. "Is that like saying you're just a little bit pregnant?"

Aiden laughed, and yep, he managed to make that sound hot, too. "It's nothing that requires meds, just some refocusing, redirecting, keeping busy. And tacos," he tacked onto that.

"Tacos?" she questioned, wanting to laugh but holding it back.

He nodded, flashed that grin again. "Tacos are usually the answer."

Before she could respond to that, their phones both sounded with texts, and she soon saw it was from Owen—who'd probably gotten less sleep than she had. The group message was to let them and the other deputies know they now had a warrant to search Brady's place and the report on Chloe's texts was in. Also, Brady, Hudson, and Wylie would all soon be in for interviews.

That was Aiden's and her cue to get moving and to cut the chitchat—if that was indeed what it was. Maybe it was flirting, but if so, it got pushed aside as they started toward their vehicles.

"By the way, maybe we should just go ahead and tackle this stuff between us head on," he said, definitely grabbing her attention. So much so that she stopped at her car and looked at him.

"The memories that keep getting triggered whenever we are around each other?" she asked. "Or the...heat?"

"Both," he confirmed.

She would have preferred that it just be the first one. Talking about the heat, well, seemed to fire it up even more.

"Tackle it how?" she wanted to know.

He shrugged in a way that only he and a *been there, done that* rock star could have managed.

"Full throttle emersion. Work side by side until we're either immune to what happened in the past or decide we can't keep our hands off each other. Maybe going out for tacos," he tacked onto that.

She couldn't help herself. Lexa smiled, and she had to clamp her teeth over her bottom lip to make it go away. "I think we're about to…" She stopped when she heard some kind of hissing sound.

And the gunshot that followed.

Aiden reacted fast, charging right at her and dragging her to the ground. Their coffees went flying from their hands. Before Lexa could even wrap her mind around what was happening, he pulled her to the side of his truck.

There was another shot, another, then more. There seemed to be a dozen of them all firing at once.

"Everyone get down," Lexa shouted to the CSIs and the people inside the manor.

She hoped they'd already done just that. Hoped, too, that none of them and no one in the surrounding area had been hit.

There were no houses or businesses directly next to the manor since it was the last building on a dead end street with empty lots all around it. The nearest occupied place was a good block away, but that didn't mean someone couldn't be venturing down this way to check out the crime scene.

Aiden and she both drew their guns and glanced around, looking for a shooter. Lexa didn't see anyone, and she couldn't pinpoint the location of their attacker. The shots were spewing out in all directions.

"Smoke," Aiden pointed out, tipping his head to a vacant lot across the street from the manor.

The owner kept the grass cut, but like at the back of the manor, there were plenty of trees and shrubs. And, yes, a fire. Or at least smoke anyway. It was rising up, thick and black, near some oaks.

"The bullets are cooking off," Aiden muttered.

Because the sound of the shots was deafening and her heartbeat was pounding in her ears, it took Lexa a moment to realize what he meant. Cooking off. As in someone had put some bullets in heat or flames, and the ammo had heated to the point of firing.

So, maybe no shooter.

But she couldn't imagine that this had been an accident. No. Someone had purposely set this. Maybe the same someone who'd tried to burn Aiden and her the night before.

That sent a slam of raw anger through her. Because the sonofabitch wasn't just endangering them but anyone around them.

The shots continued, and she heard one crash into Aiden's truck. It came too close to hitting them, but there was nothing they could do. There was no gunman they could stop with their own weapons. No way for them to run to cover because those cooked-off bullets could land anywhere.

"Everybody stay down," she yelled again in case any lookie-loos had come this way to see what was going on.

No one responded so Aiden and she waited for the gunfire to slow…and then stop.

"Don't get up yet," Aiden warned her. "There could be a stray bullet left in the fire."

He was right, but waiting was hard. She wanted to make sure the CSIs, the fire chief, and arson investigator were all right because she was pretty sure some of the bullets had hit the manor itself.

The seconds seemed to crawl by, but there were no more shots. Finally, her heartbeat settled down some, too. Enough for her to turn and look at Aiden.

And her heart went to her knees.

Because that's when she saw the blood. That's when she realized that Aiden had been shot.

——— ☆ ———

CHAPTER SIX

———— ☆ ————

Aiden ground his teeth together as the nurse stitched him up. Hell in a big assed handbasket, he hated stitches. Hated hospitals. Wasn't a fan of pain either or needles being threaded into him.

But he especially wasn't a fan of that gut-punched look in Lexa's eyes.

A look that let him know she was blaming herself for him getting shot. She was no doubt mentally playing around with *what if* scenarios to try to figure out how she could have stopped it. As if all of this was on her. It wasn't.

It was on the sonofabitch who'd set up that fire to cook-off those bullets.

Aiden was now making his mission in life to catch said sonofabitch and make him or her pay. Not because of his own injury. It was hardly more than a scratch. But because people could have been killed.

Including Lexa.

Including any damn body who just happened to be in the range of this attack.

Word had already gotten around about this

latest incident. Of course, it had. And that was the reason he had "you ok?" texts from all three of his brothers, Shaw, Declan, and Hayes.

He had texts, too, from Owen who'd used a lot more words when he'd first asked for a status report, then a follow-up one about a half hour later to check on how things were going. And finally a third text to let Aiden know he wanted to see him when he was done in the ER.

Aiden was betting at least one or two of the texts Lexa had gotten in the past hour had been from Owen as well. Maybe to try to find out if Aiden had been bullshitting him about being okay. But there'd been no BS. This was a minor injury, period, that wouldn't affect anything.

"Finished," the nurse finally declared. According to her name tag, she was Sarah Jean Barlow, and she stepped back to check her work. The six stitches on his left bicep caused by a hot bullet ripping across his arm.

Aiden had been damn lucky. An inch or two over, and it could have hit something vital, including his heart.

"The doctor will be in soon to check you," the nurse went on, gathering up her supplies. "Try not to get it wet or to do anything that'll pop the stitches. I'll see about getting you a script for pain meds—"

"Don't want them," Aiden was quick to say. He'd rather deal with the pain than a fuzzy brain caused by the meds.

Sarah Jean shrugged in a suit-yourself gesture and walked out of the treatment room, leaving Lexa and him there to stare at each other.

"I'm staying on the job," Aiden decided to clarify. "This won't affect my ability to do anything." He hoped. At least it wasn't his shooting arm, and that made this is a silver lining.

Lexa sighed, and he expected her to argue with him about that. She didn't. "If I were in your shoes...your boots," she amended, "I'd do the same thing." She paused. "Someone tried to kill us again. Why?"

Ah, that was the million-dollar question. Too bad he was a piss poor answer that was just pure speculation.

"I could be a coincidence that we were in a wrong place, wrong time deal," he offered up, "but I don't buy that. As for why?" And now came the speculation. "Maybe to try to hamper the investigation. Maybe because this asshole thinks we know something that can put him or her in a cage."

"Yes," she muttered. "That was my theory, too. That, or else one of us pissed somebody off, and that person didn't care if the other one of us becomes collateral damage."

Aiden had gone there, too. "Pissed anybody off lately?" he came out and asked.

"Not that I know of. You?"

"Not that I know of," he repeated. Their gazes stayed locked, and while he'd never thought he had mind-reading skills, he could practically feel what she was thinking. "But Mandie Trainor's parents probably don't think fondly of us."

"No," she agreed in a mutter.

Lexa groaned and scrubbed her hand over her face, and like him, she was no doubt fighting the flashbacks of that night. Of them rushing it to save Mandie.

And getting her killed in the process.

That hadn't been their plan, of course. It'd been to save her after her ex-boyfriend had kidnapped her. But shitstorms could and did happen, and that night everything that could go wrong, did. The asshole boyfriend had set a fire, nearly burning them all alive, and even though Aiden and Lexa had managed to get out with Mandie, she'd died from the injuries the asshole had inflicted on her.

Lexa and he had been too late.

No way to fix that. No real way to live with it, either. And it was no doubt the same for Mandie's parents. Which was the reason he'd brought up their name to Lexa.

"I did a quick check, and Mandie's folks are out of the country," Aiden admitted. "They're on one of those package trips across the UK. I think if they'd decided to get revenge after all this time, they'd want to be around to see it."

Besides, Mandie's parents, Margaret and Greg, had never expressed their hatred for Lexa and him in any way. Just the hurt. The pain.

Which cut way deeper than any hatred could.

"So, if it's not them, then this is almost certainly connected to Chloe. To Brady," Lexa muttered.

Yep. And that meant they were back to the theory that someone wanted to dick around with the investigation. Or silence them because they might know something. The trouble with that was Aiden didn't know squat.

Well, other than that part about Brady's PTSD.

Brady or Wylie likely wouldn't want that coming out if Brady was ever arrested for murder. But it seemed to Aiden there were other less messy and bloody ways to handle that.

So, he was back to muddling the investigation. Or...

"We both thought we saw someone when we escaped from the fire," Aiden reminded her.

"Yes," she agreed. "And maybe he or she believes we saw more than we did. Like a face. Or some other distinguishing trait we could use to make an ID."

That angle was possible. But there was another one that sprang to mind. "What if the killer wants to pile on the evidence against Brady?" Aiden threw out there. "What if this attack was meant to spur Owen into arresting him?"

She nodded and took a moment clearly processing that. "If so, that points back to Hudson."

He didn't get a chance to give Lexa his take on that because the examine room door opened, and

Dr. Millie Lopez walked in. Aiden had already met her briefly when Lexa had rushed him into the ER. She'd been no-nonsense then and continued that demeanor now as she examined the stitches, covered it with a bandage and then listened to his heart.

"All right," the doctor said, yanking the stethoscope from her ears. "You're good to go."

Aiden didn't waste any time coming off the treatment table and heading to the door. He was anxious to get back to the station, and Lexa clearly was, too, because she fell in step beside him. Quick steps that slowed considerably though once they reached the ER doors.

They both looked out, checking for any kind of threat. Aiden didn't see one, but that didn't mean squat. After all, he hadn't seen those bullets before they'd been cooked-off.

Still keeping watch, they went into the parking lot and got in Lexa's car since she'd used it to get him to ER—after he'd insisted she not call an ambulance. Aiden scowled when he saw the blood on the seat, and he made a mental note to arrange to have the car detailed.

Lexa got behind the wheel and headed toward the exit. "I've been giving some thought to your full-throttle emersion," she said, surprising him. "Uh, not *we can't keep our hands off each other* full throttle," she amended. "More like how it applies to, well, you getting shot. If someone is truly gunning for us, I'd rather you be close by so I can give backup and vice versa."

Aiden smiled. Probably not the right reaction. But he rather liked the idea of them being joined at the hip. Not because of the heat, though that was a factor, but because of the *vice versa*. Yeah, he'd gotten shot this time, but if they had a killer after them, he didn't want the asshole getting to Lexa.

"Close by," he repeated. "I'm all for that. We leave work together, go in together. We stay together."

He sort of held his breath on that last one, figuring she might nix it. She didn't. "I have a spare room at my place here in town," she said instead as she pulled into the parking lot of the police station. "That way, I can keep an eye on those stitches. Fifty bucks says you'll pop one by tomorrow."

"You're betting on me busting my stitches?" he asked.

"It's a sure thing," she remarked, stepping out.

Aiden got out, too, his gaze sweeping around as hers did, and they didn't dawdle as they made their way into the building.

He immediately spotted Owen, who was in his office but with the door wide open. And Owen saw them, too, because he motioned for them to join him.

"Status," Owen said, looking at the bandage on Aiden's arm.

"I'm good to go," Aiden assured him.

Owen studied him for several moments as if trying to figure out if that was true. He must have decided it was because he shifted into the word mode. "I just got a call from the fire chief, and he confirmed that the bullets had been cooked-off. Three boxes of ammo and a fire triggered by a timer. The fire also destroyed the area around it so there are no visible footprints."

"A timer," Aiden repeated like profanity. Because it meant the device could have been set at any time. The attacker could have been long gone by the time the shots went off.

"We're checking the security cameras around town," Owen went on. "Maybe something will turn up."

Aiden considered the location of the cams and wasn't very hopeful one of them would have captured anything helpful. The attacker might not have taken one of the roads or even a vehicle to go in the direction of the manor. That area could be accessed on foot during the night.

"I've also been going over Hudson's and Chloe's phone records," Owen went on, turning his laptop screen so they could see it. "All pretty standard stuff except for the one she sent to her brother."

Yeah, that one. *I'm so scared. I think I've made a bad mistake. I think he might try to kill me.* Definitely not standard.

"I can't see anything leading up to Chloe sending the text," Owen explained. "But what I can see if that her calls and texts to Brady significantly decreased since that argument at the bar."

"Maybe they hadn't kissed and made up the

way Brady claimed," Lexa suggested. But then she sighed. "Of course, Brady could say they hadn't been texting or calling as much since they'd been together."

Brady could indeed claim that. And it might be the truth. But it put a knot in Aiden's gut because this felt like one step closer to his friend being arrested for murder.

Owen looked at Aiden. "I saw you got the whole shebang backgrounds running on Chloe and Hudson."

Aiden nodded and hiked his thumb in the direction of his own laptop at his desk in the bullpen. "I was about to check that."

"Good," Owen muttered. "Stick with that, and use my office if you want a bigger workspace. Also, feel free to observe the interviews. Right now, I have Callie and Shaw tapped for Hudson, and I'll be taking Brady and Wylie. Separate, of course," he added.

"When are Hudson and Wylie due in?" Aiden asked.

Owen checked the time. "Brady, any minute now. Hudson, in about twenty minutes. Wylie is due in about an hour and a half. I should be done with Brady by then." His voice dropped off when there were sounds of voices in the reception area.

Aiden turned to see Brady, who was right on time, being sent through the metal detector. And he wasn't alone. Gillian Petty with him.

"Interesting," Lexa said. "He didn't bring a

lawyer with him."

No, he hadn't. Was that because Brady didn't realize just how close he was to being charged? Or maybe he had thought he could defend himself? Either way, that wasn't a good move on his part.

"I don't think he voluntarily brought Gillian with him either," Aiden pointed out after seeing the annoyed look Brady shot at Gillian.

Gillian was muttering something to Brady so maybe she didn't see the expression, but it was obvious to Aiden that Brady didn't want her there. Obvious, too, that Gillian was going away since she went through the metal detector behind him.

"Hayes and Jemma are at Brady's place now with the CSIs, carrying through on the search warrant," Owen said, moving toward his office door. "If anything pops on that while Brady is in interview, they'll let me know."

Owen went into the bullpen, greeting Brady and motioning for him to follow him. "We'll be in interview room two today."

"Can I be with Brady for that?" Gillian asked. "He's obviously shaken to the core."

"No," Owen and Brady said in unison.

Gillian flinched a little, and then quickly regained her composure. "All right, I'll wait here for you," she said to Brady. "But I wish you'd consider having your dad with you."

"No need," Brady insisted, and he headed toward the interview room with Owen.

"Brady really is shaken," Gillian muttered, not

addressing anyone in particular. "I need to do something to help him. I have to find out why this is happening." She kept her attention pinned to Brady until he was out of sight, and then she glanced around, spotted a chair just off reception and went there.

Since Aiden didn't want to say anything that Gillian might overhear, he grabbed his laptop, and Lexa and he went into Owen's office, shutting the door behind them. He dragged over a chair so Lexa and he could sit side by side as he went through the...well, lake of data.

"Good grief," she muttered. "There's a lot."

"Yeah, there usually is. People don't know what kind of cyber footprints they leave."

And in this case, there were well over a thousand footprints for each of them. Posts and mentions on social media. Uploaded info to employment sites. Newspaper articles. With that much data, he had to look for something that stood out.

"Hudson and Chloe were adopted out of foster care when Chloe was six and Hudson was four," he read.

And it seemed as if they'd had a fairly normal life with their adoptive parents before they died in a boating accident when Chloe was twenty. Before that though, Chloe and Hudson had lived in an upper middle-class neighborhood. Good schools. No hints of trouble.

"Chloe was popular in high school," Lexa

pointed out.

She was. There were hundreds of posts, photos, and mentions of her being in various clubs and receiving academic honors. Hudson had some, too, but it was nowhere close to Chloe's numbers.

"Their bio-mother, Silby Wight, was killed in a car crash nine months ago," Aiden said when he came across something else. "I don't recall Chloe ever mentioning that."

"Neither do I," Lexa agreed. "But it's possible she wasn't that close to her."

"True." And he did a side search on Silby to see what came up.

Plenty.

Aged forty-six at the time of her death, which meant she would have only been seventeen when Chloe was born. No record of her ever being married or of the father of her children. But there were other records.

Bad ones.

The woman had multiple arrests for both drug possession and DUI, and one arrest had landed her in jail for a two-year sentence. That was when her kids had ended up in foster care. Had Silby then willingly allowed them to be adopted? Or had she fought it? Aiden plugged in another search to see if anything came up on that, but it was a bust.

"Chloe met Brady and moved to Outlaw Ridge only a couple of months after her bio-mom's death," Lexa said. She paused, shook her head. "Something about that feels…off."

"It does." He had paused, too, while he continued to run the search on Silby. "But I don't see any indications that Chloe was involved in other relationships that got serious fast. So, maybe love at first sight?"

Their gazes met then, and, damn it, that blasted heat did a number on him. Apparently, it did one on her two.

"This isn't love at first sight," Lexa insisted. "It's attraction."

Yep, it was. A damn strong one. So strong that Aiden had to force his eyes off her and back onto the laptop. Thankfully, something popped up on the screen that snagged his attention and got his mind off love and lust with Lexa.

The police report on Silby's death.

Both Lexa and he moved in for a closer look. "Hell," he growled. "Silby was killed by a drunk driver. A seventeen-year-old boy named Miles Bennett."

Aiden kept reading, going through the hits that pulled up Miles's arrest. Then, the plea deal that had gotten Miles probation and community service but not one day of actual jail time.

"Miles' parents have money," Lexa said, motioning to that on the screen. An estimated wealth of three million. Like him, she continued to read the summary of the plea deal.

"Shit," they said in unison when something popped right out at them.

The name of Miles' lawyer. The attorney who'd

orchestrated the plea deal that had gotten him off. Brady's father, Wylie.

---- ☆ ----

CHAPTER SEVEN

———— ☆ ————

Lexa stood in the observation area, looking at the large monitors that provided camera feed for each of the interview rooms. Wylie, who'd arrived a half hour early, was sitting quietly at the table, waiting for Owen to finish up talking to Brady.

Callie and Shaw had already ended their interview with Hudson, and the man had stuck to his claim that Brady had murdered his sister. Of course, other than that one text from Chloe, Hudson didn't have any proof of that.

The man had also seemed totally shocked when Callie had brought up his bio-mom's death and he claimed not to have known about it, that he hadn't seen her in years. Hudson had also insisted he hadn't been aware that Brady's father had been connected to that plea deal that had kept his mother's killer out of jail.

Lexa had no idea if Hudson was telling the truth, but so far nothing had come up to dispute anything he'd said.

It was the same for Brady. He, too, had seemed surprised when Owen had brought up Wylie's connection to Chloe's late mother, and Brady had claimed that Chloe never mentioned her bio-mom. So, the woman's death might not even apply. It might be one of those odd coincidences.

But Lexa hated coincidences.

And this one didn't feel right.

The door behind her opened, and she turned to see Aiden. After the interviews had started, they'd decided to split duties, with him finishing up the background searches on Hudson and Chloe and with her observing the questioning of their persons of interest.

"I hope you've found out more than I have," she remarked.

Aiden shook his head and moved to stand beside her so he could also see what was on the monitor. "No social media posts from Chloe or Hudson about their bio-mom."

"And Hudson denied knowing about her death," Lexa provided.

On the screen, she saw Owen finishing up with Brady, telling the man he could leave but that he was to stay available to answer any other questions that might come up. Brady practically sprang to his feet and hurried out ahead of Owen who then headed to the interview room with Wylie.

Lexa listened as Owen fed in the pertinent data for the recording, and he then sat across from the man.

"How's my son?" Wylie immediately asked.

"I've finished with the interview, and he's free to go," Owen answered, and that caused Wylie to visibly relax. Not for long though. The tension ratcheted up again when Owen added, "For now."

Wylie muttered some not so muffled curse words. "Brady's a wreck, and I don't want him pressured. You have no evidence against him, and you shouldn't be treating him like a suspect."

"Means, motive, and opportunity," Owen reminded Wylie, holding up three fingers. "Brady has all of those. I have to consider him a suspect. I'd be derelict in my duty if I didn't, and you know that."

Wylie groaned, a loud, almost feral sound that was loaded with anger and frustration. "I believe Chloe's alive. I think she set up her own death so that Brady would be arrested for her murder."

That got their attention—both Aiden's and her and Owen's.

"And why would Chloe do that?" Owen came out and asked.

Wylie wasn't so quick to answer this time, and he glanced around the room as if buying him some thinking time before he finally looked at Owen again. "Because she's pissed at me. Because she's so enraged at me that she wants to punish me through Brady."

"Is this about Chloe's bio-mom?" Lexa muttered.

But Owen didn't question Wylie about that particular subject yet. He just waited for the man to continue.

"I know in my gut that Chloe doesn't love my son," Wylie finally said. "So, shortly after they announced their engagement, I went to her and offered her money, a hundred grand, to break up with Brady, leave town, and never contact him again."

Lexa was sure she looked surprised because she was. She glanced at Aiden to see if he'd known anything about that, but he shook his head.

"And, no, Brady didn't know anything about it," Wylie went on. "If he'd found out what I'd done, he would have been furious, but he also would have been safe from whatever that woman had in store for him."

"I'm assuming Chloe didn't take the money?" Owen wanted to know.

"She did not." Wylie spat out each word like profanity. "But I tried again to press her to take it during that phone call you found out I made to her. Again, she turned me down because I believe that no amount of money is worth her giving up on revenge."

"Revenge?" Owen leaned back and folded his arms over his chest. "Does that have anything to do with her mother's death?"

Wylie's eyes widened, and he seemed to do some sort of mental double take. Then, he sighed. "Of course, you'd find out about that."

"I had deep searches done on those connected to Chloe. Including you. I know you were the lawyer for the young man who killed her biological mother. Care to explain that?" And Owen sounded all cop now.

Wylie sighed again. "I don't want Brady to know any of this." He stared at Owen and cursed. "You told him?"

"I asked him if he knew about Silby Wight and Miles Bennett. He said that he didn't."

"Did Brady ask why I'd agreed to defend Miles?" Wylie blurted the question, and there was now some panic in his tone.

"No," Owen replied. "I think he was, uh, trying to process the info when I ended the interview." He paused a moment. "Why did you defend Miles?"

Wylie made another of those sounds of frustration. "Because his mother is an old friend of mine, and she begged me to take the case."

"And you didn't know Silby was Chloe's mother?" Owen asked.

"No," he insisted. "Brady hadn't even met Chloe at the time, and Silby had a different last name."

Owen pinned his gaze to Wylie's. "But you found out later."

Wylie nodded. "I learned it about a month ago when I had a PI run a background check on Chloe. The adoption came up, and the PI was able to give me the birth mother's name. That's when I realized that Chloe must be up to something. I figure she wanted to punish me for defending the client who killed her birth mom, Silby Wight."

"Chloe would have had to have been close to

her mom to want that," Owen remarked. "Was she?"

Wylie shrugged. "The PI didn't find anything about that, but she must have been. That's what this staged death of hers is all about."

Owen stayed quiet a moment, no doubt giving that some thought. "There was a lot of blood in the manor," he finally pointed out.

"Blood that Chloe could have stockpiled and used to set Brady up." Now, Wylie was the one who paused. "Or me...shit...she could have planted something to make me look guilty." He took out his phone. "I need to have a conversation with a lawyer friend. Could you give me a minute?"

Owen obliged, getting to feet. "Interview paused while subject speaks with a lawyer." He gave the time and the verbal command to turn off the audio before he stepped out.

Aiden opened the door to the observation room, and Owen stopped, glanced inside at the monitors. "Did anything else turn up on Chloe or Hudson?" Owen asked.

"No," Aiden answered. "Neither seem to have many friends, and they aren't exactly partiers. Most of their social interaction is with each other. Well, they were before Chloe got engaged to Brady anyway. What I don't know is how Hudson took it to suddenly not being the center of his sister's world. Did he retaliate? Did he come up with a plan to kill her? Or are Chloe and Hudson together in on whatever the hell this?"

"Yeah," Owen said in such a way to let them know he was considering any and all of those possibilities. He glanced at the monitor again. "Keep an eye on Wylie. I need to call and hassle the lab about those blood results. If Wylie asks where I am, tell him I'll be back in about twenty minutes. That should give him enough time to talk with his lawyer."

With that, Owen shut the door and left them to it. Since there was now no audio in the interview room, the only thing they could do was watch. And what they saw was a very agitated Wylie pacing while he spoke on his phone.

"Everything Wylie said could be true," Aiden commented, breaking the silence that'd settled between them. "Chloe could have set this up."

Lexa made a sound of agreement. "But if so, she had to plan it for months. That's a long time to put up a façade, especially if she had to pretend to love a man she might actually hate."

"The hatred could all be for Wylie," Aiden pointed out. "Punish the father by using the son."

True, that would be the deepest cut for a loving parent, and Wylie did love his son. "Still, that doesn't rule the obvious here. That Brady and Chloe argued. She tried to end things, and he ended her." Then, she went with another theory. "I also think we need to consider someone else who lost the center of their world when Brady and Chloe got engaged. Gillian."

Aiden's nod was quick, which let her know

he'd already considered it. "With the wedding just hours away, Gillian might have decided the only way to keep Brady was to get rid of the bride."

Yes, so several different motives could be playing into that. And Brady could truly be innocent.

"That look we saw on Brady's face when he arrived at the manor and since then—that shock could be because he's worried sick about the woman he loves," Lexa speculated.

Again, Aiden's nod was quick, and he took out his phone. "I'll text Owen about questioning Gillian."

He sent the text, and within seconds Owen sent back a reply. "Hell. Will do."

The *hell* was no doubt frustration over them adding a fourth person of interest to their list of Wylie, Brady, Hudson, and now Gillian. Actually, there were five if Chloe was still alive and had orchestrated this.

Lexa made her own sound of frustration that had Aiden shifting toward her. He frowned. Then, winced, and it took her a moment to realize the movement had pulled at his stitches.

"The numbing junk the nurse put on it is wearing off," he let her know, frowning at the bandage on his arm.

"I can get you some over-the-counter pain meds," she insisted, and Lexa went for the door handle.

But he stopped her. Unfortunately, he stopped

her by putting his hand overs hers, and mercy, mercy, mercy, even that packed a wallop.

She looked up at him, just as he looked down at her. Their eyes sort of collided and held. Just held. With them making some serious eye contact. That, too, packed another wallop.

"You know if I kiss you, that's it," he drawled. "No turning back."

Lexa couldn't help herself. She smiled. "One kiss and we have sex?"

"Well, not immediately. Not here for sure. But it'd be a kiss we wouldn't just enjoy and forget."

She eased her hand from his and cocked her head to the side. "You must be sure of your kissing abilities."

He shook his head. "I'm sure of *yours*."

She laughed. And he captured her laugh with a kiss.

A soft touch of his mouth to hers. So light it was barely there, but it was indeed scorching. The heat seemed to seep right through her.

Aiden didn't press harder. Didn't deepen it. Didn't go in for anything more than just this. Just this one incredible way of turning every inch of her into a puddle of need.

After a couple of moments of that sweet torture, Aiden eased back and met her gaze again. "Thought I'd get that first kiss out of the way."

She shook her head to try to clear it. No luck. "You kissed me even after you said there'd be no turning back from it."

"I was wrong," he admitted. "There was already no turning back even before the kiss."

Ah, that. Lexa wished she could disagree. But she couldn't. Nope. Being with Aiden, becoming his lover, seemed inevitable.

That thought was flashing like neon in her head. The sound of his phone beeping chased the thought away and snapped her out of the daze. Her attention flew back to the monitors, where she saw they hadn't missed a thing. Wylie was still pacing and on his phone.

"It's the security system at my house," he relayed to her. "Apparently, someone or something triggered a sensor in the pasture."

Aiden clicked the function on the app to bring up the camera feed, and Lexa moved closer to take a look. It wasn't the grainy image that she'd been expecting from a security system but high enough quality for her to see an amazing view of the picturesque Texas Hill Country. There was a barn surrounded by acres of green pasture, and beyond that, white limestone bluffs.

What she didn't see was anything that could have triggered the system.

Not at first anything. Then, Aiden zoomed in on one of the massive live oaks. And she saw something.

The woman who was peering out.

Chloe.

───── ☆ ─────

CHAPTER EIGHT

———— ☆ ————

With Lexa right beside him, Aiden hurried toward the front of the police station. And nearly smacked right into Owen.

"Chloe's at my place," Aiden quickly told him, and he showed him the camera feed.

"Hell," Owen spat out. "Go there now and take a cruiser. I'll arrange for backup."

Aiden grabbed a set of the cruiser keys from the wall pegs just inside Owen's office, and Lexa and he ran out of the building and into the parking lot. They didn't waste any time getting inside the cruiser, and Aiden sped away. They needed to get to Chloe before she left.

But what the heck was she doing there?

Maybe if they got to her in time, they'd be able to get that answer from her. For now though, Aiden was mentally going back to the theory of Chloe faking her own death. The woman was certainly alive and looking well on his phone screen so that theory could damn well be true.

"I'll put the camera feed on the dash," Lexa said, taking his phone and pairing it with Bluetooth.

Within seconds, the feed appeared on the much larger monitor. Aiden could still see Chloe, but she was no longer standing. She had stooped down and was using her hands to rake away some leaves from the base of a tree.

Aiden continued to volley glances at Chloe while he drove out of town and toward the place he'd bought after he'd gotten out of the military. A former ranch that definitely wasn't on the beaten path. In fact, his nearest neighbor was nearly a half mile away. Which meant Chloe almost certainly hadn't stumbled onto the place by accident.

"I don't see any injuries on her," Lexa remarked.

Aiden made a sound of agreement. No injuries, but he also couldn't see what she was doing either. She was still hunched down but had shifted so that her back was now to the camera.

"Has Chloe been to your place before?" Lexa asked.

"A couple of times with Brady," Aiden said, trying damn hard to recall if she'd asked anything about his security system then. He was sure she hadn't because that would have sent up a mental red flag for him. "Chloe didn't do or say anything suspicious. She definitely didn't seem to be scoping out the place to do whatever the fuck she's doing right now." And, yeah, there was frustration in Aiden's voice.

Lexa nodded and kept watching. "What about the cameras? Would she be able to see them so she could try to avoid them showing what she's up to?"

"No, the cameras are well hidden," Aiden assured her.

He'd made sure of that.

Working for Strike Force meant he'd sometimes made enemies. After all, bad guys didn't like to be caught and have hard justice served up to them. And Aiden had wanted to be certain that he would get a warning if one of the assholes tried to sneak onto his property. He just hadn't expected the person who was currently doing the sneaking would be his good friend's missing fiancée.

At least Chloe wasn't dead, and that meant Brady and their other suspects were off the hook for murder.

Well, maybe.

"Try to zoom in on her face if she turns around," Aiden instructed Lexa.

"You think it might not be Chloe?" she immediately asked.

"It sure looked like her." Aiden paused and let the worst-case scenarios fly. "But it could be someone posing at her. Someone that her killer hired to make us believe she's alive."

"Like Brady or Wylie," she said on a sigh. "Or Gillian."

Yep. But of the three, this seemed more like something Wylie would do. This way, Brady would be off the hook for murder, and if Wylie had indeed killed Chloe, then it also got her out of his son's life.

On the screen, the woman still didn't look

directly at the camera, but she shifted again, and Aiden got a glimpse of what he thought she might be doing.

"That's ammunition and some kind of device," he muttered. "I think she's setting up a spot for a fire and cooking off more bullets."

That caused some alarm to shoot across Lexa's face. "How far is that from your house?"

"About a hundred yards. Bullets can definitely do some damage from that distance. And she might be planning to set more than one."

But it seemed a strange way to try to kill someone. If that indeed was her intention.

A more direct approach to killing them would be to lie in wait on the side of the road and shoot at them as they drove by. That came with risks though. Risks that the vehicle would be bullet resistant, which the cruiser would be. And lying in wait meant Aiden potentially spotting and identifying the shooter. Chloe, or whoever the heck this was, wouldn't want that.

At the reminder that someone could indeed be near the road and waiting to ambush them, Aiden continued to look around. The problem was there were too many damn places to hide. This was the Texas Hill Country after all, and nature was in abundance.

They were still three miles from his place when Lexa's phone rang, and she frowned when she looked at the screen. "It's from an unknown caller," she said. "I don't usually answer these."

But she took this one on speaker, no doubt because she thought it might be connected to their investigation. And it was.

"Deputy Mullen," the man said the moment he was on the line.

Hudson.

Her frown deepened. "How did you get my number?" she asked.

"It was in my sister's contacts," he snapped out, his words rushing together. There was also a frantic edge to them. "I need to know what's happening. I was on Main Street at the diner, and I saw two Outlaw Ridge cruisers flying out of the parking lot. Did you find Chloe?"

"I can't discuss an active case with you," Lexa told him.

"Did you find my sister?" he shouted, and this time, there was more than just an edge of anxiety. "Oh, God. Did you find her body?" The question dissolved in a hoarse sob.

"When and if we find anything that I can share with you, I'll let you know," she replied. "In the meantime, just go home."

"I'm not going home," Hudson snarled. "I'm following the second cruiser."

"Shit," Lexa grumbled under her breath. "Don't do that, Hudson. You could put people in danger."

Yeah, including himself if any of that cooked-off ammunition went his way. His vehicle likely wouldn't be bullet-resistant.

"If she's dead will you finally arrest the

sonofabitch?" Hudson went on, clearly ignoring everything Lexa had just said. "Will you finally put that bastard fiancé of hers in jail?"

"Go home, Hudson," Lexa repeated. "If you come near the cruisers, you'll be arrested for interfering with an investigation."

The line went dead, and on a huff, Lexa texted Owen to let him know that Hudson might be on his tail. Hopefully, Hudson wouldn't get in their way, especially if those bullets started flying.

Aiden took the final turn toward his house, maneuvering the cruiser onto the narrow dirt and gravel road lined with trees. It was also a steep incline since his house was basically in a valley. Below them, he had a bird's-eye view of the house, the pastures, and the tree line where the woman was still fiddling around with something on the ground.

On the monitor, Aiden saw her head suddenly whip up. Probably because she'd heard the cruiser's engine. She didn't waste any time standing. But she didn't run. Didn't hide.

Just the opposite.

She came away from the tree and started running across the pasture toward his house.

"She's keeping her head down," Lexa pointed out.

Yeah, she was. Maybe that was intentional so they wouldn't be able to tell whether or not this was Chloe. But it was also possible she was just watching where she was stepping.

"If she's set off a timer on that ammo, she's taking a huge risk by being out in the open like this," Lexa muttered.

Again, he agreed with that, and Aiden made his way down the hill, pulling to a stop in front of his house. Since the woman was still too far away for him to get a closer look at her, he just kept watching the monitor.

And he saw her stop.

Again, her head snapped up, and she made a sweeping glance around her, taking in the cruiser. Maybe taking in something else, too.

"What does she have in her hand?" Lexa asked, zooming in on that.

It was hard to tell, but Aiden thought it might be a large cell phone or...hell, some kind of detonation switch.

"Don't get out of the cruiser," Aiden instructed and continued to watch the woman.

She looked at the thing she was holding. Looked at them, too, keeping her head angled in such a way that it was hard to see her entire face. Then, she turned and started racing back toward the trees.

Damn it. He couldn't let her get away.

Aiden threw open the cruiser door. Lexa did the same. "Stop," she shouted to the woman. But she continued to run, sprinting into the cover of the trees and disappearing.

It was a risk to go after her, but he didn't need to spell that out to Lexa. She'd been a cop long enough to know what could happen here. If the bullets started, they'd have to get down.

Lexa and he raced toward the fleeing woman, darting around the side of his house.

Just as all hell broke loose.

CHAPTER NINE
———— ☆ ————

Lexa heard the strange whirring sound a split-second before something dropped onto the ground just ahead of Aiden and her.

"A grenade," Aiden spat out, already pulling her away it.

Good thing, too, because it exploded, the blast thundering through the air and knocking them backward. If Aiden hadn't had hold of her, she would have almost certainly fallen hard on her ass. As it was, they staggered, thankfully regaining their footing.

And they ran.

Not a second too soon either. Because another grenade landed in the yard right next to the house. Obviously, someone was using a launcher, and Lexa couldn't tell if it had come from the direction of where they'd seen Chloe. It was possible the woman had moved.

Or someone else was trying to blow them to bits.

Aiden and she reached the side of the front porch, and they ducked down behind some thick shrubs. Definitely not bulletproof, but it was better than being out in the open.

Lexa glanced around, trying to figure out their options. Such that they were. They were a good twenty feet from the cruiser, and if they tried to get to it so they could escape, they'd be out in the open for way too many steps. Easy targets. But they could be equally easy to get at here, too, if the launcher sent another grenade their way.

She glanced up at the porch. It was elevated about three feet off the ground. Great. That was thirty-six inches or so of levering themselves up while, again, they'd fall in that easy target zone. Still, she knew that was their best shot, and Aiden obviously agreed with her.

"We need to get inside the house," Aiden muttered, using his phone to access his security system and no doubt open the door. "Text Owen and let him know what's going on."

God. She hadn't even thought of that, but if Owen and Shaw—and yes, even Hudson—arrived now, they could be driving straight into a blast. The cruiser might not withstand a direct hit from a grenade, and Hudson's vehicle certainly wouldn't either.

Lexa hated that her hands were trembling when she typed out the text, but she managed to send the warning to Owen when there was another sound. Not an explosion this time.

But gunfire.

And lots of it.

Just like at the manor, the bullets started popping off. Dozens of them. All at once, seemingly coming at them from every direction. It took Lexa a moment to realize that there was no *seemingly* to it.

The bullets were indeed coming from all four sides at them.

Chloe or someone else must have set multiple fires to cook-off the ammo, and they hadn't used a couple of boxes this time. No. There were hundreds of shots going off at once.

"How the hell did someone get this close to my place to set up this shit?" Aiden snarled. And judging from his tone, he'd be finding out the answer to that as soon as he could.

Lexa was betting the culprit had stayed just far enough away from Aiden's security system to arrange for this attack, and then...what? Had Chloe or her lookalike shown herself to lure them here?

Maybe.

But there could be something else entirely going on. Now though, wasn't the time to think about that before Aiden shifted, ready to move.

"Go fast," he told her. "I'll be right behind you."

She didn't respond. Lexa simply got moving. And she went damn fast. She caught onto the side of the porch, levering herself up and scrambling to get out of Aiden's way so he could do the same.

The bullets just kept coming, and hell in a handbasket, it was loud. So loud that it seemed to rattle her bones. The noise was certainly rattling her nerves, along with giving her the motherlode of a really shitty flashback.

Not now. Not now. Not now.

The mantra worked, some, but so did her sheer will just to get to the front door. After all, because he was behind her, he wouldn't be getting to safety until she was inside.

It felt like an eternity for her to scuttle across that porch, and the gunfire wasn't making it easy. A bullet smacked into the wall just above her head. Another hit the porch inches from her. But what wasn't happening was another explosion, and she held her breath that they'd get in before there was another one.

The moment she reached the door, Lexa threw it open and dived in. Aiden was only a heartbeat behind her, and he kicked the door shut. "Geralt," he called out. "Secure the house. Full measures."

"Done," the automated voice replied.

Immediately, locks began to snick and what appeared to be metal shutters lowered over the windows. Outside, a siren went off. A pulsing wail with a threat and urgency to it. It drowned some of the shots and was probably designed to get an attacker running.

"Geralt," she repeated, mouthing the words since he might not be able to hear her speak. "You named your security app after *The Witcher*."

He nodded. Considering the nightmare that was going on around them, it surprised her that she was amused by that. It seemed to surprise Aiden, too, that she had recognized the character's name.

"Stay low," he instructed, "just in case there's another grenade blast."

She certainly hadn't forgotten about that possibility, but she followed him, crawling away from the door and into a large open-plan living, dining, and kitchen area. He led her to a stone fireplace which was likely the safest place if there was indeed another explosion.

"Geralt, put feed from all security cams on monitor one," Aiden called out.

The landscape painting on the wall opposite them dissolved into a split-screen view of eight different cameras. Lexa tried to pick through them all, frantically looking for whoever was doing this. But she couldn't see a person. Only those blasted bullets ripping through whatever they hit. The trees, the shrubs. Even chunks of the limestone on the exterior of the house.

"Geralt, zoom in on cam six," Aiden ordered.

It was the area by the trees where they'd first spotted Chloe. But Lexa couldn't see her there now. However, she could see the small fire that was no doubt fueling some of this gunfire.

Her phone rang, somehow managing to cut through the godawful noise, and she saw Owen's name on the screen. She showed the screen to Aiden who immediately issued a command.

"Geralt, lower volume on sirens."

The sirens throttled down just enough for her to have this much needed conversation. "We're at the end of the road to Aiden's," Owen said the moment he was on the line. "Status."

Lexa bit back the first word that came to mind. *Shitstorm.* But that's what this was. Still, Owen would need specifics.

"Someone fired two grenades at Aiden and me," she spelled out. "And bullets, probably cooked-off, are flying every damn where." As she said that, some struck against the metal shutters. "We lost sight of Chloe, but she ran into the woods where there's one of the cook-off fires."

"Are you two hurt?" Owen asked.

Lexa looked at Aiden. And cursed. Because there was blood oozing out from beneath his arm bandage. He'd likely popped a stitch or two. Cursing some more, she reached in her pocket for a tissue. Of course, she didn't have one so she used her sleeve to swipe away the blood.

"We're not injured," Aiden replied.

Lexa huffed, and continued clearing away the blood, but she didn't dispute what Aiden had just said. She would have done the same thing had Aiden's and her situations been reversed.

"My advice is for you to stay put until the bullets have cooked-off and I've tried to locate whoever launched those grenades," Aiden added to Owen. "I'm viewing camera feed now."

"Good," Owen said after a couple of moments of hesitation. Was he doubting that whole *we're not injured* stuff? Probably. "Keep me posted. Hudson's here, and I need to stop him," he added, ending the call.

Lexa hoped Owen could manage to do that. And she had no doubts that her boss would also check to see if Hudson had been the grenade launcher. After all, they only had Hudson's word for it that he'd been in town when he'd seen Aiden and her speeding out in the cruiser. Chloe's brother could have been here lying in wait the entire time.

"Geralt, continue zooming in on cam six," Aiden instructed.

The app wasted no time doing that, and the resolution of the feed was good, considering how far from the house this was. But the zoom showed more of the fire. More of those bullets being fired.

And maybe something else.

Lexa wanted to get up and go closer to the screen, and judging from the way Aiden leaned forward, he wanted to do the same. But his attention was focused where hers was.

Just beyond the fire.

In the shadows created by the thick canopy of trees, there was…something.

"Maybe a fallen limb or some shrubs," Aiden muttered.

Yes, that could be it. But it could also be a person. Someone crouched down. Someone watching the place.

Outside, the bullets finally began to slow, and it occurred to her that the person in the shadows could be waiting for the shots to die down before firing another grenade at them. Lexa wasn't sure she wanted to know if the house would withstand a direct hit like that.

"Geralt, launch the drone," Aiden said. "Send it to area six, just behind the fire. Engage the lights on the object in area of the three o'clock feed."

Lexa was sure she goggled at him. "What does that mean?" she had to ask.

"Watch," he said, keeping his own attention pinned to the monitor.

Moments later, she saw the drone, and she guessed it'd been launched from somewhere on the roof. It went straight to area where they'd seen that possible figure. And, yeah, lights lasered out of the drone, quick pulses that zinged through the air, landing in the area just beyond the fire.

"The lights aren't lethal," Aiden said. "Not death rays or anything like that. But they can distract and alarm someone into moving."

They watched. But the object didn't move.

"Geralt, engage the camera on the drone," Aiden instructed. "I want a close look of the target."

The drone adjusted. So did the monitor, and the drone feed soon appeared there. It wasn't as clear as the camera footage had been, but there was still enough resolution. The drone moved slower now, scanning over the object.

Which wasn't an object at all.

Lexa saw the body. And then a face.

Hell.

It was Chloe.

───── ☆ ─────

CHAPTER TEN

———— ☆ ————

With his security shutters now rolled back up, Aiden sat in his kitchen, looking out the wall of windows at the chaos of what was now essentially a twelve-acre crime scene.

Usually, this was where he had his morning coffee and processed whatever Strike Force assignment that he'd just finished or was about to start. It was where he stood sometimes just to admire the amazing Texas Hill Country. That view from these windows was the reason he'd bought this house.

But at the moment, the view sucked.

And he was hurting. Bad.

The pain was from the popped stitches that were in the process of being cleaned and redone by the EMT, Brent Mendez, that Owen had sent to the house. Hell's Bells. It felt as if the EMT was cleaning it with battery acid. But at least this ordeal would be over soon. He hoped. The chaos happening in and around his house would likely go on for hours or even days.

There was a team of CSIs combing the

grounds and the surrounding woods, looking for any evidence that would help the cops piece together what the hell had happened. In their white protective suits, the team looked like ghosts haunting the place. They crept along, gazes sweeping around while they gave the ME folks a wide berth.

Because they were loading the body on a stretcher so it could be taken to the medical examiner's van and then to the morgue.

Since Aiden and Lexa had made the trek down to those woods shortly after the gunfire had stopped, they had gotten a good a look at the dead woman. And they could both confirm it was indeed Chloe. Hudson had confirmed it as well with a photo that Owen had shown him. So, there was no doubt to her identity.

But there were questions.

Boatloads of them.

Other than the single gunshot wound to the head, Chloe had no other injuries. Not a cut, not a scratch. Not even a bruise. Which, of course, didn't make sense in light of the bloody mess that'd been left at the manor. And now on his property.

And that's where the questions started.

At first, Aiden had thought that maybe Chloe had been shot with one of the bullets that'd cooked-off in the fire. But the ME had noted there was stippling around the wound which meant the shot hadn't come from a distance. This had been an up close, and judging from the angle of the shot, the ME believed she'd been shot while partially facing the barrel of the gun.

Why had Chloe allowed someone dangerous to get near her like that? Or had the person sneaked up on her, and then she'd turned to face them right before the shot had been fired?

Yep, too many questions and not nearly enough answers.

Part of Aiden wanted to be out there with the CSIs, searching for something. For *anything*. But Owen had had a different notion about that. His boss had wanted Lexa inside, chasing down reports, and Aiden to be treated for the popped stitches before he started scouring through any images that the drone might have captured when it'd been flying over the area where Chloe's body had been found.

Aiden glanced over at Lexa, who was indeed attempting to chase down reports and results. She was on hold with the lab that would hopefully soon give them some answers. She had her phone sandwiched between her shoulder and her ear while she, too, stared out the window and watched the activity of the crime scene.

She looked exhausted. And no doubt was. Spent adrenaline was a pisser to deal with, and it could cause the fatigue to seep right into your bones. It was the reason Aiden was chugging a Coke and was hoping like hell that it'd give him the energy boost he needed, along with maybe taking the edge off his throbbing arm.

Torn stitches could be a pisser, too, but the EMT finally finished up and declared the job *all done* before he gathered his things. He didn't issue Aiden any warnings as the nurse had done. Maybe because Brent knew him and figured he'd be wasting his breath. Aiden didn't want to tear the new stitches, but he couldn't be careful to a tee when it was obvious that someone wanted Lexa and him dead.

Brent gave them a wave and headed out, and the moment the EMT had shut the door behind him, Aiden voiced the command to Geralt to engage the locks and rearm the security system. No need to risk someone trying to sneak inside, and it'd be easy to do with all the people coming and going.

Because of the activity on the grounds, Aiden had shut down the motion sensors on the grounds while the CSIs and ME were working. That would prevent the alarms from going off every few seconds. However, he had left the security cam on at the top of the road to alert him if anyone else arrived.

Aiden turned in his chair, opened his laptop that he'd put on the counter, and loaded the drone feed so he could start picking through that. Emphasis on picking. Drone feed wasn't that clear, and there was the added problem of the tiny camera maybe not being aimed where it needed to be. Still, the footage had to be reviewed, frame by frame.

He started, making it through the first hundred or so images, and finding nothing, when he saw movement from the side windows of his breakfast area. Like the ones in the kitchen, these had been designed to capture more of those views, but from this angle, he could also see the vehicles.

Lots of them.

Two cruisers, the ambulance, the ME's van, and the CSIs' SUVs and trucks were still parked there. Ditto for Hudson's car.

According to one of the updates Aiden had gotten from Owen, Hudson had insisted on staying at the scene until Chloe's body was on the way to the morgue. Owen had agreed, but Aiden suspected that was because it gave him a chance to question the man.

At the moment though, Owen wasn't doing any questioning. Not to Hudson anyway. He wasn't in sight, but Owen was in front of his cruiser and was having a conversation with the head CSI, Quentin Radford.

"Yes, I'm still here," Lexa said when someone came on the line. She stayed quiet, obviously doing a lot of listening, and whatever she was hearing had caused her forehead to bunch up. "You're sure? Never mind," she quickly amended. "Of course, you're sure. Could you please let Sheriff Striker know?" Another pause. "Thanks," she added, ending the call.

Lexa sighed. "The lab confirmed that the blood at the manor belonged to Chloe."

Well, that was interesting. "Have they tested the blood for additives? Because if she drew her own blood and stockpiled it so she could toss it around and stage an attack, she'd have to put in an anticoagulant."

Lexi nodded. "They tested it, and the additives were there." She stopped and fired off a text, no doubt to Owen, to let him know the results. "Normally, they wouldn't look for something like that, but they did under the circumstances."

Yeah, they would. Owen would have pressed for it. "Other than to fake her own murder, I can't think of a reason for Chloe to do all of this."

Lexa made a sound of agreement. "And that means she did it to set up Brady. Or Wylie. Maybe both."

That's what he figured, too, and if so, the motive could be the death of her mother. Chloe could blame Wylie and want to strike out at him through Brady.

"Brady," Aiden muttered, getting to his feet so he could stretch. "I'll have to call him soon."

First though, he'd need to let Owen inform Brady of Chloe's death and then re-interview him again. Because even if Chloe had faked her death, it wasn't a fake now. And since there'd been no gun found near her body, it meant she hadn't taken her own life.

So, someone had murdered her.

Who and why were yet more of those unanswered questions, but Aiden had yet another one to add to this puzzle.

"Why come after us like this?" he asked. "Wylie's at the police station. Or at least he was right when you and I left. That's a solid alibi. He couldn't have been the one to kill Chloe."

She nodded, reached over took his Coke and had a sip before she handed it back to him. "Maybe Chloe intended to plant some evidence that Wylie had hired someone to do this." She paused, cursed. "And he could have."

Yeah. But Aiden was having a hard time wrapping his head around Wylie wanting to kill him. He was Brady's friend, and as far as Aiden knew, Lexa hadn't been a threat or enemy to Wylie. So, that brought him back to Chloe.

"Chloe could have set all of this up," Aiden spelled out. "Murder me and the lead investigator on her disappearance. Stir up outrage and fear in the town to pressure Owen into arresting Brady, Wylie or both."

"But then something about this sick plan went wrong, and Chloe was murdered," Lexa finished for him. "If she had help putting this together, perhaps the person decided he or she couldn't trust Chloe. Maybe it was Hudson or a hired gun."

That theory worked for him, too. But he had another one. "If Brady found out Chloe was alive, he would have had time to get here and take her out. So would Gillian."

Lexa snapped toward him and reached for her phone. "I need to let Owen know to check and see if

Gillian has an alibi." She fired off a text and within seconds, she showed Aiden the thumbs up emoji she got from Owen.

They both turned back to the window, and from the corner of his eye, he saw Lexa shudder a little when the medical examiner's team started moving the body toward the van. He knew for a fact that Lexa had seen at least two other dead bodies, but it never got easier.

"I owe you fifty bucks," he said, and Aiden waited until she'd turned to him before he pointed to his stitches.

That earned him a very brief smile, followed by a much longer frown. Her gaze slid over the fresh bandage before it lifted and met his eyes. There was definitely exhaustion in those baby blues.

But that got shoved aside.

When the heat stirred there instead.

He saw the frustration that caused her, and it probably didn't help that she had such recent memories of that kiss back at the police station. Nope. Didn't help. Because it was needling away at him too.

Aiden set his Coke aside and went to her. The moment he reached her, he pulled her into his arm. The one that wasn't stitched. He kissed her, the kind of kiss he'd been wanting from her for months.

And it didn't disappoint.

The taste of her slammed through him, and he immediately wanted more. So much more. This was playing with fire, and the fire was winning.

Aiden wanted it to win.

He wanted to keep kissing Lexa until it led to a whole lot more. For now though, the kiss was more than enough. Scalding hot. Deep. Perfect. Lexa made it even better by hooking her arm around his neck and pulling him even closer to her. Her breasts landed against his chest, and his chest liked that very much. So much so that it shot up the heat even more.

Adjusting their position and mindful of his injured arm, he turned her so she was anchored against the kitchen island, and that allowed for even more of that body to body contact. Of course, a certain part of his body, his brainless dick, was pressing for the end of foreplay and some full-blown sex.

The sound of an incoming text put him and his dick on hold.

"Fuck," he muttered.

The corner of her mouth lifted in a smile. "Nope. Saved by the text."

That brought on his own smile, which went south pretty damn fast when he saw it was from Owen. And the content of the message.

"Owen says that Hudson wants to use the bathroom and claims he can't wait until they get back to town," Aiden relayed. "He wants to know if it's okay to bring him here because he doesn't want Hudson taking a leak anywhere on the crime scene."

Aiden sent back an "OK" reply, and, nudging aside that urge to kiss Lexa, he headed for the door. "Geralt, disengage security on the front door." The locks clicked, and Aiden opened it.

It didn't take long for the cruiser to pull to a stop in front of the house, and Owen and Hudson exited. Hudson walked almost robotically behind Owen, and the man's face was a mask of shock.

Or maybe fake shock.

It was hard to tell, but if Hudson hadn't been the one to kill his sister, then he was likely stunned by her death. But just in case this was all an act, Aiden would keep a close eye on him. Or rather his security app would.

"Geralt, monitor our second guest at all times," Aiden instructed.

There were no cameras in the bathrooms, but the app would make sure Hudson didn't go anywhere else in the house and would also do a body scan in case Hudson decided to grab something in the bathroom and use it as a weapon.

When Hudson reached the foyer, he slid glances at both Lexa and Aiden. "Did you kill my sister?"

Aiden didn't respond and motioned toward the powder room just off the hall. After tossing out a glare, Hudson stormed in that direction.

"You think he could have murdered Chloe?" Aiden asked Owen.

Owen lifted his shoulder. "So far, there's nothing to indicate that, but it's possible.

Something could have happened with Chloe's plan. Something to piss Hudson off. Like this. I found it when I demanded to see any recent calls or texts he'd gotten."

He took out his phone and showed Lexa and him a picture of a text. It was from an unknown number to Hudson.

"*I'm sorry*," Aiden read aloud before he looked at Owen. "You think that's from Chloe?"

"Could be," Owen replied. "The CSIs didn't find a phone near Chloe's body."

Lexa and he had seen Chloe holding something on the camera footage, but that had turned out to be a detonator for the fires.

"They also haven't found the vehicle that Chloe used to get here," Owen added a moment later, "and a phone could be inside it. Hell, lots of stuff could be in it. I doubt Chloe thought she'd be murdered when she came here."

True, and Chloe almost certainly hadn't walked far to get here, especially not carrying the amount of ammo used in the cooking off fires. It was likely she'd parked nearby and made her way through the woods. Of course, another possibility was that Hudson or someone else had dropped her off. If so, there'd be no vehicle, and therefore no evidence, in the area.

"Hudson claimed that he thought the text was from someone who had the wrong number," Owen continued. "And he didn't reply. At least, he didn't with this phone, and if he used a burner, it's not in his car. He agreed to let me search it."

No need to point out that Hudson could have discarded the burner on the drive over. Owen would have already thought of that possibility.

Aiden heard the bathroom door open, and Hudson made his way back to the foyer. "She's dead, and no one is being punished for that," the man muttered. Anger flashed through his eyes. "You should have arrested Brady. You should have never given him the chance to get to her."

There were so many things wrong with that asshole comment that it took Aiden a moment to figure out where to start. "A couple of minutes ago, you accused Lexa and me of killing your sister."

"You could have helped Brady. You're friends with that sonofabitch."

And there it was, the possible motive for why Hudson would want them dead. In Hudson's eyes, a friendship with Brady was an unholy alliance.

"Are you forgetting that Chloe faked her own death?" Owen asked.

That took some of the fire from Hudson's eyes. "I'm sure she had her reasons for doing that."

"Yeah, and the reason was to set up Brady for something he didn't do," Lexa supplied. "Did you help her to that, Hudson? Did you help your sister with any part of her plan?"

"No," he spat out. He started to stay something else but then seemed to change his mind. "I loved Chloe, and now she's dead."

"Like your bio-mother," Aiden said, testing the

waters to see if Hudson would react.

And he did.

There was another flash of anger. Too intense for Hudson's claim that he hadn't been close to his biological mom. But the man quickly shut it down and hurried out of the house and toward the cruiser.

"You hit a nerve there," Owen commented. "Good. I'll see if I can press it again." He glanced at both of them, his gaze combing over their faces. "Was your security system damaged in the attack?" Owen asked.

Aiden shook his head, already aware of where this was going. "I can work," he said as a preemptive strike.

"I'm sure you can, but I want both of you to have some downtime," Owen insisted. "How close are you to being done with the images from the drone?"

"Close. Maybe another half hour," Aiden replied.

"Good. Go through it, and then take the rest of the day off." Owen shifted to Lexa. "I can give you a ride back to your place if you think you've got good enough security."

Lexa did some glancing of her own then, starting with Owen and her gaze settling on Aiden. "I'd like to stay here if you don't mind."

"I don't mind," Aiden couldn't say fast enough.

The relief came. So damn much of it. If Chloe's killer wasn't finished with them, Aiden didn't want Lexa facing down the SOB alone.

"Good," Owen said, sounding relived as well. He turned to leave, but his phone rang, stopping him inches from the door. "It's Declan," he said.

"Declan, I'm with Lexa and Aiden," Owen let him know. "And you're on speaker."

"They'll want to hear this," Declan was quick to say. "I've been studying the feed from the town's security cams, checking to see who might have been heading to the manor around the time that fire was set. And I might have found something. I'm sending a photo to you now."

Within seconds, Owen's phone sounded again, and the picture began to load.

"This particular shot was taken from a recently installed doorbell cam of the house just two blocks away," Declan explained. "I've checked, and I can't find a logical reason for her to have been out there on this street at that time of night."

Aiden and Lexa both leaned in to check out the "her" that Declan was referring to. And they soon saw the woman driving straight toward the manor.

Gillian.

———— ☆ ————

CHAPTER ELEVEN

---- ☆ ----

Lexa studied the footage of the doorbell cam that Declan had sent Aiden and her. The images were far from clear, thanks to the lack of street lights in this section of town and the distance between the cam and the car as it'd driven by. But by freezing the frame as Declan had done, it was easier to zoom in and see the woman's face.

"Gillian looks furious," Aiden commented. He was seated at his desk in his home office with Lexa right next to him in the chair she'd pulled over.

"She does," Lexa said. "But we don't know if that anger prompted her to set the manor on fire."

Dragging in a long breath, he made a sound of agreement. "The person who started that fire had gas cans. And maybe also set up the device for those cooked-off bullets."

Something like that took planning and wasn't a spur of the moment reaction fueled by rage. But it could have happened, especially if the rage had been going on since Chloe and Brady's engagement.

"Gillian could have brought those items with her," Aiden continued. "Maybe with the intentions of...what? Murdering Chloe?"

"That'd be my guess. Gillian could have learned that Chloe would be there, and she might have decided to end her life then and there. First, set the fire. If Chloe managed to get out as we did, then the bullets might finish her off." Lexa stopped, shook her head. "But then why continue to come after us?"

And a theory came to mind.

"When we climbed out of that window at the manor, we both thought we saw someone," she reminded Aiden. "If it was Gillian, she possibly believed that we recognized her and were building a case against her. She could have wanted to take us out before we managed to arrest her."

Aiden nodded, but he didn't seem completely convinced. Neither was Lexa. There were just too many missing pieces of this particular puzzle, and they needed Gillian to fill in the blanks. And hopefully that would happen soon.

Owen had tried to call her a couple of times, but Gillian hadn't answered. In fact, the calls had gone straight to voicemail. There might be a good reason for that, but Aiden could think of a couple of bad ones.

The woman was on the run.

Or she could be dead.

After all, if someone was cleaning house by

murdering Chloe and attempting to kill Lexa and him, then Gillian might be a target, too. That could be especially true if Chloe's killer believed Gillian could expose him as the killer. If so, that led right back to Wylie and Brady since they had almost daily contact with Gillian. Either man could have heard or saw something that put Gillian on the defensive.

But that could mean Gillian was ready to kill Brady.

And Lexa couldn't see the woman going there. Then again, she hadn't seen the façade Chloe had put on for six months.

A green light on his computer monitor flashed and then alerted them that there was incoming footage from the police station. Aiden minimized the image of Gillian on the doorbell cam and pulled up the live feed from the interview that Owen had just started with Brady. One look at Brady and Lexa knew that he'd already been informed of his fiancée's death. Brady wasn't crying, but his face was a mask of pure grief.

Well, maybe.

Again, Lexa didn't want to believe the worst, but she knew people faked stuff all the time. Especially killers. And the bottom line was that Brady had a motive to kill the woman if he believed that she'd tried to set him up for her murder.

"Brady, for the record can you tell me where you went after you left the police station this morning?" Owen asked.

"I, uh..." Brady stopped and scrubbed his hand over his face. "Did Chloe suffer when she died?"

It was an interesting question and could be taken two ways. One, as the concern for a woman that Brady had loved. Or hope that she had experienced some miserable pain after what she'd done.

"The ME is examining her body now," Owen said. "We'll know more details of her death after the postmortem."

"But you saw her," Brady insisted. "You would know."

Owen shook his head. "She'd been shot. That's all I can tell you."

Brady groaned, leaned his head back and stared up at the ceiling for a moment. "I didn't go anywhere after I left here," he said, finally answering the question. "I just drove around, trying to sort out my thoughts. Trying to figure out what happened to Chloe."

"And you had no inkling that she'd stockpiled her own blood?" Owen pressed.

Brady's attention snapped back to the sheriff. "I'm still not sure she did that. Yes, I know what you told me. That the blood wasn't fresh, that it had some kind of additives in it, but there has to be an explanation about that."

Owen shrugged. "Like what?"

"I don't know." Brady groaned, but then it seemed as if he'd had a lightbulb moment. "A couple of months ago she went to the blood drive at the hospital here in town. She has one of those rare types. AB negative. So, someone could have stolen her donation."

"And why would someone have done that?" Owen wasted no time in asking.

This time the frustration came when Brady smacked his fist on the table. "I don't know," he repeated.

Another of those theories popped into Lexa's mind, and she took out her phone to get started on a search of the exact date of the hospital's blood drive. After she had that info, she'd check to see if there had been a theft or break-in reported.

"You're thinking someone could have stolen the blood," Aiden said, "and then used it to stage Chloe's death and implicate her in the arson that nearly killed us?"

"Yes," she verified. "Of course, that wouldn't explain the motive for doing that. I mean, if they wanted Chloe dead, why not just kill her? Still, maybe the plan wasn't to kill her but to get her arrested and locked up."

The words had barely left her mouth when there was a series of three sharp beeps. "Vehicle has turned onto the road," Geralt informed them.

That didn't put Aiden or her on full alert. Not yet anyway. It could be more CSIs or another deputy. Still, they went to the front window to check. Owen, Hudson, the ambulance, and the ME's van had already left, but the CSI vehicles and one cruiser were still there.

The car, a black Audi, slowed past those vehicles, maybe checking to see if there was anyone inside. There wasn't. The two deputies and the CSIs were in the area where Chloe's body had been found.

After a few seconds, the Audi driver accelerated again, and when it got closer, Lexi finally got a look at the driver. Apparently, so did Aiden.

"That's Gillian," he grumbled. "What the hell is she doing here?" he muttered, taking the question right out of her mouth.

And the answer was Gillian was apparently coming to see him because the woman stopped her car in front of his house.

"Geralt, scan our visitor for weapons," Aiden instructed as Gillian made her way to the front door. Not a slow pokey stroll either. She was practically running up the steps while her gaze flew all around her.

"Visitor is not armed," the app announced just as Gillian rang the doorbell.

"The app is pretty good at detecting conventional weapons," Aiden let her know. "But I've learned the hard way that just about anything can be used to hurt someone. And I have the scar to prove it."

Lexa had no doubts about that, and she wouldn't be taking any chances with Gillian either.

"Geralt, disengage security for only the front door," Aiden instructed. "And unlock it."

When the locks made that clicking sound, Lexa slid her hand over the weapon in her shoulder holster. Aiden did the same before he opened the door to their visitor.

"Is she really dead?" Gillian blurted. She didn't try to barge her way in, and the woman actually took a step back when she saw they had their palms resting on their guns. "Is Chloe really dead?"

Since Chloe's next of kin, her brother, had been notified of her death, there was no reason for Lexa to hold back on answering that. Besides, she wanted to see Gillian's reaction.

"Chloe is dead," Lexa spelled out.

Gillian reacted to that, not with shock but rather anger. "Fuck, fuck, fuck," she spat out, pressing her hands to both sides of her head. "You're going to arrest Brady for this, aren't you?" But she didn't wait for them to respond. "Well, you shouldn't. Brady didn't do this."

"And how would you know that?" Lexa asked.

Gillian glared at her. "Because I know Brady. So do you."

The words stabbed out, heavy with emotion and accusation that Aiden and she should believe Brady was innocent because of their friendship.

Groaning, Gillian began to pace across the porch. "If you arrest Brady, that means Chloe's real killer goes free."

Obviously, the woman just couldn't accept that Brady might be guilty. Was that because Gillian had been the one to kill Chloe?

Lexa decided to test those waters.

"The sheriff's been trying to get in touch with you," Lexa said. "Since you're here, I'll go ahead and give you the Miranda Warning."

Gillian stopped pacing, gasped, and pressed her hand to her heart. "So, now you believe I killed that gold-digging bitch?"

All right. Now, they were getting somewhere. All that ranting emotion meant the woman might say something she might not normally reveal.

Lexa recited the Miranda while Gillian's glare and profanity got a whole lot worse. When Lexa was done, she hit the record button on her phone and went with her first question.

"Why were you near the manor last night when the fire was set?" Lexa demanded.

Gillian's glare finally went south, replaced by surprise. And maybe fear. "I didn't set that fire," she said.

"That's not an answer," Aiden pointed out. "Why were you there?"

The woman took her time answering, and she must have found another stash of mad because the anger returned to her eyes. "I heard Brady mention that Chloe would be at the manor so I went there to have it out with her, all right? I was going to demand that she leave Brady alone. I was going to write her a check, giving her every penny in my savings if she'd just leave."

Interesting, since Wylie had tried to pay Chloe off, too.

Aiden made a circling motion with his hand for Gillian to continue. "I didn't even see Chloe," she insisted. "Her car wasn't there, and no one answered at the manor when I knocked."

Lexa made sure her gaze and her voice were all cop. "You were pissed so I can't believe you didn't at least try to find her. Did you look around the back of the manor?"

There was a small parking area there for staff, and for Gillian to get there, she could have passed right by the window of the dressing room.

"I didn't," Gillian said without a whole lot of conviction. She stopped, huffed. "I got a little spooked. I, uh, thought I saw someone lurking around the back so I got back in my car and went home. A few hours later, I heard about the fire at the manor."

"Describe the person who saw lurking around," Aiden told her, and he sounded like a cop, too.

Gillian shook her head. "I only got a glimpse. And it might have been nothing. Shadows," she concluded.

"Any reason you didn't volunteer this info to the cops?" Lexa asked.

She huffed again. "Because I didn't want questions like this. I didn't want the cops hounding me the way they are Brady. Neither one of us killed Chloe. From what I'm hearing, she tried to set up Brady."

It didn't surprise Lexa that gossip about that was already getting around. But it was also possible that Gillian hadn't heard the talk but rather had firsthand knowledge of what had happened at the manor and here at Aiden's.

"Where were you for the past three hours?" Lexa added a moment later.

"Home. I was working." Gillian stopped. "Then, Wylie called to tell me that Brady had been brought back in for interrogation and that Chloe's body might have been found."

Again, not a surprise. Wylie was Gillian's boss after all, and he probably wasn't happy about his son being questioned. But was he happy about Chloe's death?

Maybe.

But if so, Wylie still hadn't personally been the one to kill her.

"Here's what I want you to do," Lexa spelled out. "You're to drive straight to the police station and give a thorough statement to the sheriff. Don't leave out anything. This is a murder investigation, Gillian, and you can be charged if you withhold evidence."

Oh, the woman did not like that. "Fine," Gillian snapped, and turning on her heels, she hurried back to her car.

"Geralt, engage locks and security," Aiden said after he shut the door.

From the window, Lexa watched Gillian drive away, and she took out her phone to text Owen to let him know the woman was on her way to the station. That way, if she didn't show, Owen could send someone after her.

"I want to look at the feed from the doorbell cam," Lexa muttered, sending a second text to Declan. "I'd like to study it frame by frame to see if I can spot this mystery person that Gillian, you, and I might have seen outside the manor."

"Good idea," Aiden said, heading back to the kitchen. "I need to finish looking at the drone feed."

He woke up his laptop, and she saw the images that he'd already pulled up. Since it might take Declan a while to get her the doorbell footage, she moved next to Aiden and watched as he accessed the next round of the feed.

Her body instantly reacted to the close contact, reminding her of that kiss they'd shared right here before Hudson had shown up. She cursed because she could almost feel the heat zinging back and forth between them.

Lexa forced herself to focus on the screen. That got a little easier for her when Aiden zoomed in on one of the images. It wasn't a shot of Chloe's lifeless body or even the fire that'd ignited when the bullets had started going off. No, this was something beyond that.

At first, it just looked like a pixelated blob. A swirl of gray and green shadows. But as Aiden zoomed in more and enhanced the image, she could make out that it was a man dressed in jeans and a gray shirt. He appeared to be in mid-stride, running.

Aiden went to the next image and this time, he was immediately able to enlarge the blob, and she could make out more of the man's features.

"Shit," Lexa said on a groan.

The man on the feed was Brady.

———— ☆ ————

CHAPTER TWELVE

———— ☆ ————

Aiden had had a serious debate with himself about this trip to the police station. A debate that had involved Lexa as they basically decided to ignore Owen's order that they get some rest.

Downtime could wait.

What was more important now to both Lexa and him was being there when Owen confronted Brady with the feed from the drone. Images that showed that Brady was right there, right when Chloe had been shot.

Of course, Lexa and he wouldn't actually be in the interview room, but depending on the info that came out, Aiden wanted to have a word with Brady afterward. Especially if Brady ended up being arrested for murder.

They stepped into the side entrance and immediately spotted Owen in the hall just off his office. He was having what appeared to be a tense conversation with Wylie. Not a surprise. Wylie wouldn't be pleased about his son being held for yet more questions. And Owen likely hadn't told Wylie the reason for this latest interview. Owen would want to spring that on Brady first so he could gauge his reaction.

"You've got Gillian here, too," Aiden heard Wylie snap. "What the hell do you think she did?"

Owen sighed. "You know I can't get into that with you. And Gillian didn't request a lawyer when she came in." He patted Wylie on the arm. "Why don't you go on home or to your office? Once Brady and Gillian are done, I'm sure they'll contact you."

That didn't do squat to lessen the anger tightening Wylie's face, but the man did walk away, heading for the front door.

Owen doled out another of those sighs when he shifted to Lexa and Aiden. "You two could have viewed the interview on your laptops." He waved off any response they would have given. "But I understand why you're here."

"Have you shown Brady the drone photo yet?" Lexa asked.

Owen shook his head, and he took out a manila envelope he'd had tucked under his arm. "I had a few of the shots printed out, and I'll ask him about them in a minute or two. Right now, he's being swabbed for gunshot residue. I didn't have to get a warrant for that," he added. "Brady agreed."

Maybe Brady had done that because he had nothing to hide. Then again, he could have worn latex gloves. The drone images hadn't been clear enough to show that on his hands.

"What about Gillian?" Aiden wanted to know. "Did she give you anything new from what she said on the recording that Lexa sent you?"

"Nope," Owen replied. "She stuck word for word for what she told the two of you. She also consented to a GSR test. Ditto for Wylie. And, FYI, both of those came back negative. The only one of our suspects who wouldn't voluntarily consent was Hudson."

"Interesting," Lexa commented.

"Yeah, I thought so, too," Owen said. "He claimed he wasn't going to cooperate with the cops who wouldn't arrest his sister's fiancé for killing her."

Aiden could practically hear the man spewing that out. And it might all be genuine grief and anger over his sister's death. But it could also be because he'd been the one to kill Chloe. The trouble with that?

Motive.

Wylie, Brady, and Gillian had that in spades. But so far, nothing had come up about Hudson that would make him the frontrunner of suspects.

Owen turned when he saw Jemma come out from the adjacent hall. She held up the small evidence bag, indicating that the GSR test was done.

"I'll let you know the results," Jemma told him.

Apparently, Owen didn't plan on waiting for that because he headed toward the interview room. Aiden and Lexa went into observation, where he saw Brady on the screen. He was frantically typing away on his phone, but he stopped the moment Owen stepped in.

"I didn't kill Chloe," Brady immediately insisted. "The GSR test will prove that."

No, it wouldn't. Aiden knew that the presence of GSR wasn't a given even if the person tested had recently fired a gun. A strong gust of wind, the right kind of soap or even the angle of the shot could affect it.

Owen didn't address what Brady said but instead recited the pertinent info for the recording. After he'd finished that, Owen sat across from him and looked him straight in the eyes.

"Brady, tell me where you went after you left our earlier interview," Owen said.

"Home," he answered without hesitation.

Owen opened the envelope and spilled out the photos taken from the drone feed. Aiden watched as Brady leaned in, his gaze scanning over them. He muttered a single word of profanity, groaned, and buried his face in his hands.

"Explain why those pictures prove you were at the scene of your fiancée's murder," Owen demanded.

Brady slid his hands from his face but didn't respond right away. In fact, he paused so long that Aiden thought he might lawyer up. Which was what he should be doing, considering those photos.

"Right after I left the station," Brady finally started, "I got a call from an unknown number." He took out his phone, accessed something on the screen and slid it across the table to Owen. "It was Chloe. At least I think it was."

Owen took Brady's phone, no doubt verifying the call. "What do you mean you *think* it was her?"

"It was her voice. I'm sure of that, but it was... off." Brady paused again. "I was just so relieved she was alive, and I started asking her where she was, what had happened, was she all right, but she started talking right over me as if she hadn't heard me. And she said if I wanted to see her that I should come to the woods behind Aiden's house."

"And you didn't think to tell the cops about this?" Owen asked when Brady stopped.

Brady frantically shook his head. "Chloe told me to come alone, that she couldn't trust the cops. She also said she was scared, that someone was trying to kill her. Then, she hung up. I tried to call her back, but she didn't answer. So, I got in my truck and drove straight there."

"Then, what?" Owen pressed when Brady fell silent. "I'm assuming you went in armed?"

"Of course. The woman I love told me she was in danger, and I wanted to protect her. I failed." Brady's voice cracked on that last word. "I parked on a trail just off the road. You can't drive to that spot, so I walked. And when I got there, I saw her." He shuddered. "She was dead."

"How do you know? Did you touch her?" Owen

asked.

"No. I could see she was dead. Then, before I could even think about what to do, bullets started firing. I panicked. Flashbacks," he muttered, but it was still loud enough for Aiden to hear. "I, uh, have PTSD. Gunfire triggers it. And it triggered it bad. I remember starting to run, but then I must have blacked out. I woke up on the ground. Don't know how long I'd been there, but I got up, went to my truck and drove home."

"You left the woman you love behind?" There was a boatload of skepticism in Owen's tone.

Brady nodded, dropped down his head until his chin was practically on his chest. "Once my head cleared, I got to thinking about Chloe's call, and I believe it could have been a recording spliced together. The cadence was wrong. I didn't see that at first. I only thought about getting to Chloe. But now, I think someone used it to lure me there."

"Who would do that and why?" Owen asked.

"I don't know why. But the who could be the person that killed Chloe." He lifted his head and looked at Owen. "It's not my dad. He wouldn't have put me in a situation like that. A situation where I could have been killed."

"Wylie wouldn't have risked Brady's life," Aiden muttered. "Not intentionally."

Lexa made a sound of agreement. "So, we could be looking at two things here. Chloe could have set up that trap, maybe to lure Brady there so he'd die. But then someone killed Chloe. Wylie could have done that part."

"Yes, he could have, especially if he found out that Chloe had been playing Brady and intended to set him up."

"Go over all the details again," Owen told Brady. "And I want to know where you went after you left those woods. I also want to examine the gun you had with you."

Aiden was ready to listen to a repeat of Brady's account so he could see if he'd missed something. Or if he could detect a lie. But his phone rang, and he frowned when he saw the name on the screen.

"It's Dispatch," he told Lexa, taking the call on speaker.

"Aiden," the dispatcher greeted, and he recognized the voice. Burt Winters. "You got an incoming call from your neighbor, Orville Langston."

"Orville," Aiden muttered. What the heck did he want?

One of the other deputies had checked on the man shortly after the shooting to ask if he'd seen anything suspicious in the area. Orville claimed he hadn't and then had ordered the deputy off his property. That wasn't a surprise since Orville wasn't the friendly sort, and Aiden had only met the man once when one of Orville's horses had broken the fence and gotten onto Aiden's land.

"Put the call through," Aiden instructed Burt, and it didn't take long before his neighbor came on the line.

"Brodie," Orville greeted in his usual snarly tone. "You're gonna need to come out to my place, but I don't want you bringing a whole bunch of cops with you. Don't want them trampling all over."

"Why do you want to see me?" Aiden asked.

"Fuck, I don't want to see you. I don't wanta see any damn body, but I found this dark blue Ford Focus parked on a trail at the back ass end of my place. It's all tucked away like somebody didn't want it to be seen. Well, I saw it, and I want it gone. That's my land."

Everything in Aiden went still. Those trails weren't on the beaten path, and they ran behind Aiden's property as well. This could be the car Chloe had used.

"Did you get the license plate?" Aiden asked.

"Yeah." Orville spewed it off to Aiden as if doing so was the ultimate annoyance.

Lexa immediately used her phone to plug in the numbers to the database. "It's a rental," she let him know.

"You're gonna want to come and get this car," Orville went on.

Yeah, Aiden intended to do just that. "Did you see anything inside the vehicle?"

"I got eyes, don't I? So, of course, I saw stuff. There's a purse in the front seat and a cardboard box in the back. I recognize the box. It's from Hannigan's way out near Kerrville."

"Hannigan's," Aiden repeated. It was one of

those large sporting goods stores. And it sold ammunition.

"On it," Lexa muttered, using her phone again, no doubt to try to contact someone from the store who might be able to confirm if that's where Chloe had bought the bullets used in those cook-off fires.

"Orville, did you go inside the car?" Aiden pressed.

"I did not. It was locked, but here's my way of looking at it. It's on my land so that'll make it mine if somebody don't come and claim it real fast. Got that?" he snapped.

"I got it," Aiden assured. "My partner and I will be out there soon."

"Does this car belong to the woman that I heard got killed at your place?" Orville asked.

"Maybe," Aiden admitted. "Why? Have you seen the vehicle before?"

"No, but I saw the woman a month or so back. She wasn't on my land then. Or on this trail. She was by that little creek that runs between your place and mine. That's county land."

Aiden had to mentally shake his head. "Did you tell that to the deputy who questioned you earlier today?"

"I did not," the man blurted. "He just showed up here, and I didn't know who the hell he was."

Aiden huffed and had to get his teeth unclenched. "When exactly did you see her?"

"Like I said, about a month ago. A fox has been prowling around my chickens so I went looking for it. I was cutting through the woods when I heard her talking, and it was obvious she wasn't very happy. So, I kept quiet and got closer to see what was going on. She was pacing on the banks of the creek and pitching a right ol' fit to somebody on the phone."

"Did you hear the conversation?" Aiden couldn't ask fast enough.

"Parts of it. She was going on about payback and justice, and she said some shit like, *You will help me. You owe Mom that after what you let happen to her.*"

Aiden pushed a little harder on that. "You're sure she said just Mom and not *my mom*?"

Orville didn't hesitate. "She didn't put a *my* in there. Nope, and once or twice when she was ranting, she said the name of the person she was talking to. She didn't say it fondly either. And the name was Hudson."

———— ☆ ————

CHAPTER THIRTEEN

———— ☆ ————

Lexa drove the cruiser away from the station while Aiden waited on hold with San Antonio PD, a call that she hoped would answer a huge question. What had Chloe meant in the conversation that Orville had overheard?

You owe Mom that after what you let happen to her.

Unfortunately, Hudson wasn't doling out any answers about that because once again, he wasn't responding to the attempts for Owen to contact him. Considering Hudson was out on bail, he definitely shouldn't be ignoring the cops.

But then if he was a killer, he might be on the run.

So, a lot of attention was now being focused on him.

The other person who was getting attention was Aiden's neighbor, Orville, and Owen had made it clear he wasn't over the moon about Aiden and her going out to see the man. But Aiden had been insistent that Orville wouldn't talk to them if they brought along a hoard of cops.

Of course, they could get a warrant so they could retrieve the car and arrange to have it taken in for processing. However, that could rile Orville, and he might just clam up or refuse to make an official statement about the phone conversation he'd overheard. If he did that, they could charge Orville with obstruction of justice, but they needed his statement to build a case against Hudson.

So, after much going back and forth, Owen had decided to try to appease Orville and get both his account of what he'd heard and his cooperation in retrieving the car. That meant sending Aiden and her to get a statement from the man and for them to take a look at the car to find out if there was any evidence that would clear up some things.

But Aiden and she wouldn't exactly be solo.

Despite Orville's insistence they come alone and Owen agreeing to cooperate with the man's wishes, Shaw and Declan would make their way through the woods between the two properties. While they would stay out of sight, they'd be ready in case fast backup was needed.

"Yes, I'm still here," Aiden said to the person he had on the line. "No, I really need to speak to the officers who arrested Miles Bennett. Have them call me first chance they get."

Sighing, Aiden ended the call and glanced over at her. "The two cops are dealing with a domestic dispute that turned very ugly. It might be a while before they contact me."

That was too bad. Aiden had already done a search of the arrest record for Miles', and there hadn't been a mention of either Chloe or Hudson. However, it was possible that something had come up about them, and the info hadn't made it into the reports.

"The arresting officers might not have known that Silby was Chloe and Hudson's mother," Aiden went on. "But if Orville is right about what he heard, then Chloe blames her brother for some part of that. I'm just not seeing it. Yet. Miles, Hudson, and Chloe all lived in San Antonio but nowhere near each other."

"Hudson's a bartender," Lexa pointed out. "And Miles had been drinking when he killed Silby."

"Yeah, already checked that angle," he said, which didn't surprise Lexa one bit. She knew Aiden was thorough. "Hudson has never been charged or cited for serving underage drinkers, and his boss insists that they card everyone who orders a drink in the bar. That doesn't mean it didn't happen, but I can't place Miles anywhere near that bar. Or Hudson and Chloe."

She heard the frustration in his voice. Felt it continue to simmer inside her. They needed proof to back up Orville's statement, and if they didn't find it, then they were going to have to figure out a way to get Hudson to confess.

"Maybe Owen will have better luck speaking to

Miles," Lexa muttered.

And that would hopefully be happening soon. When Aiden and she had left the station, Owen had been in the process of trying to call Miles' parents so he could set up a phone interview.

"Why wouldn't Chloe just go after Miles instead of Wylie?" she asked as she mulled that around.

"She could have planned to do that. After she took care of Brady. Since everyone would believe she was dead, she might have believed she could get away with murder."

True, especially if Chloe set it up as some kind of accident. Or pinned the blame on Hudson. That would kill two birds with one stone. Unfortunately, the plan might still be in place if Chloe had an accomplice. Owen would no doubt warn Miles and his family about that possibility.

For now though, Lexa had to push that aside and keep watch as she threaded the cruiser on the narrow, curvy road. Aiden was watching as well, but he was also texting with the car rental company to get some kind of verification that Chloe had actually rented the vehicle. If she hadn't, if someone else had rented it for her, then that could be the accomplice.

Which, in turn, could be the person who'd murdered her.

"It's the manager at Hannigan's Sporting Goods," Aiden relayed to her when he got another text. He read it and tapped an attachment. "He just sent me a photo from their security cam. It's Chloe."

He lifted his phone and showed her the grainy image. It took Lexa a couple of glances to realize it was indeed her. Chloe had stuffed her long hair underneath a baseball cap. Maybe to disguise herself?

"She bought the ammunition four weeks ago. Two cases of five hundred rounds each," Aiden explained, glancing through the message again. "And she paid cash."

"A thousand bullets," Lexa said, giving that some thought. "It seems like more than that were fired at the two sites."

Aiden shrugged. "She could have purchased other cases elsewhere. Because she didn't buy the timers and detonators for the fires here. She could have gotten more bullets when she got those." He stopped, pulled in a breath. "She doesn't appear to be under duress here in this photo. No one seems to be forcing her to buy this much ammunition. So, that likely means this was her plan, that she wasn't simply drawn into it."

Lexa had to agree, especially in light of the conversation that Orville had overheard. So, who had killed her? Again, they didn't know, and it brought them full circle back to their suspects. Brady, Wylie, Hudson, and Gillian.

She went past the private road to Aiden's house, and it wasn't long before she came to a small creek that Lexa estimated was about twenty feet wide. The whiskey-colored water was moving fast, slashing against some embedded boulders, but it didn't seem to be that deep.

There was a clearing beneath a cluster of oak trees that would be easy to access from the road. It was no doubt where Chloe had parked when Orville had spotted her, and Lexa could understand why Chloe might not have noticed Orville. Beyond the area where Chloe would have been, there was an area of thick cedars and sage bushes with yet more trees. Orville could have stepped behind any one of them, and they would have been wide enough to conceal him.

"Why would Chloe come here?" Lexa muttered, though she already had an idea about that.

And Aiden voiced it. "She could have been scoping out my place. You can see it through the trees. Chloe might have wanted to make sure she could lure Brady here, to a familiar place where she could either kill him or further set him up to make it look as if he'd murdered her."

"Chloe *did* lure him here," Lexa picked up where Aiden left off. "And she had the added bonus of having us around." She paused. "But maybe we weren't the targets. Maybe it was always just Brady."

"Yes," Aiden agreed. "It's possible Chloe hadn't intended to kill us at the manor either. If the cleaning lady had seen the blood, she would have reported it, and soon it would have been all over town. Brady would have come running since he knew Chloe was supposed to be there. The fire and the bullets in that cook-off could have been meant for him."

Though Lexa hated to think of the people who could have been hurt or killed, including Aiden and her, with Chloe's sick plan to murder Brady, she was still tamping down her anger about that when she spotted the house ahead.

It was nothing like Aiden's well-kept place. There was yellowing, scabbed paint on the exterior. Several boarded up windows. Knee-high weeds in the yard, such that it was. What it did have that Aiden's didn't was a huge fence. It looked like something more suited for a prison than a residence.

She pulled into the driveway and immediately spotted the man at the gate. He was in his late sixties with a pot belly beneath his stained shirt and jeans. Orville, no doubt. He studied them for a moment with intense, wary eyes before he opened the gate and motioned for her to drive in.

"He doesn't have a criminal record, and I personally have never had any trouble with him," Aiden muttered. "But let's watch our six. Not just for him but in case Chloe's killer is still around."

Lexa would do just that.

She parked ,stepped out, and sized up Orville while he did the same to her. "Orville, this is Deputy Lexa Mullen."

"I know who she is," Orville said. "I keep up with the news. She's one of the city cops brought in after the old sheriff and everybody else got killed."

That about summed it up. A lot of cops had been brought in after most of the police force had been massacred.

"Let's get this done then," Orville insisted, motioning for them to follow him.

Lexa expected the man to pepper Aiden and her with a lot of questions, especially since he had likely heard all that gunfire during the attack. But he didn't. Orville didn't say a word as he had them trudge through the weeds, rocks, and uneven ground to the back of his property. There, they went through a back gate and essentially into the woods.

"This is all Orville's property," Aiden pointed out. "His land butts up to this side of the creek. My land starts on the other side of it."

It was definitely remote by anyone's standards, but she soon saw an old ranch trail. They were common in this part of Texas, and while some were hard to walk, this one was fairly level.

"How would Chloe have gotten a car out here?" Lexa asked. "Wouldn't she have had to cross the creek?"

"Not if she'd approached it from the north," Aiden explained. "There's a bridge, and from there, she could have followed a trail that would have brought her here."

"And then she would have walked to your place?" Lexa questioned. "It wouldn't be easy to wade through a creek while carrying a case of ammo. What would a case weigh?"

"About thirty-five pounds," he was quick to provide. "So, she might have had to make a couple of trips. And as for wading through water. There are parts of the creek where the water is only a foot or two wide and only ankle deep. " Aiden shook his head. "But how the hell would she have known about it?"

"I figure it was those damn ghost walking tours," Orville griped. "The library sets them blasted things up, and sometimes they go to that bluff folks call Lover's Leap. The idiots think it's haunted. It's ain't, but idiots will be idiots. Anyway, if she did that tour, she'd been able to see the start of this trail."

Aiden glanced at her. "You know about these tours?" he asked.

Lexa nodded. "I went on a Halloween one when I was a teenager to a ghost town about five miles from here. I don't recall Chloe ever mentioning that she went on one though."

Still, that would be easy enough to check, and she took out her phone to text a friend of hers who worked at the library. In under a minute, she had a reply.

"Chloe did go on one of the tours, shortly after she moved to town," Lexa let Aiden know. "And it was to Lover's Leap."

So, she had likely been planning her death and these attacks even then. Probably before she'd even met Brady. Because Lexa was thinking that meeting hadn't been an accident. Chloe had probably set it up so she could start doling out what she considered justice to Wylie.

Lexa's attention shifted to the right when she caught a flash of the sunlight glinting off something. Her first thought was this was a gun. And the start of another attack. But she soon realized it was the trim on the car that was parked right on a curved part of the trail.

Since the license plate was facing her, she could see that it matched the one Orville had given them.

"I want to see if there are two sets of footprints or one leading away from the car and toward my place. Did you walk on the trail that way?" he asked Orville as he motioned to the trail on the other side of the vehicle.

"Yeah, I went up a little piece. Just up to that tree." He pointed to an oak just past the car.

"We'll need to look beyond that," Aiden muttered. "And maybe take an imprint of his shoes to rule him out."

Yes, they would, and she hoped the man would cooperate with that and not make them get a warrant.

When they approached the car, they looked inside it. Just as Orville had said, there was a purse on the front seat and a Hannagan's box on the back. It made her wonder why Chloe hadn't stashed these things in the trunk in case anyone did some walking by.

Maybe because she hadn't planned on being

gone that long. But there could be something else in that truck. Something that Lexa would want to take a look at.

"Orville, wait here," Aiden told him, no doubt so the man wouldn't leave more footprints.

Aiden and she walked ahead. They stayed off the trail, walking along the sides, and both of them studied the ground.

She definitely saw two sets of footprints, and Lexa gauged one of them to be about her size. So, probably Chloe's. The second set was likely Orville's because they stopped at the tree that Orville had pointed out.

"What the hell is that?" she heard Orville say. Lexa turned to see the man heading toward the trunk of the car. "There's something sticking out. I didn't notice that before."

"Stay back," Aiden shouted.

But it was too late. Orville had already stepped toward the trunk.

Just as the car exploded.

———— ☆ ————

CHAPTER FOURTEEN

☆

Every muscle in Aiden's body seemed to be aching, and judging from the way that Lexa was moving when she got two Cokes from his fridge, she was experiencing the same thing.

They each had a variety of nicks, scrapes, and bruises as well when the impact from the blast had knocked them off their feet and hurled them to the ground. But all in all, they'd been damn lucky.

Orville hadn't been.

Aiden had known that from the second of the explosion. Orville had been right on it. Hell, had probably stepped on it or triggered something that'd set it off. And it'd killed him.

Soon, his body, or what was left of it, would be on the way to the morgue, but for now, the county bomb squad was combing through the woods to make sure there were no more explosives that could end up killing or injuring the crime scene investigators and cops.

Shortly after Lexa and he had gotten out of

those woods, Owen had ordered them to go to the hospital to be checked out. They had, and after all kinds of tests, they'd been medically cleared and given the suggestion of taking a long, hot soak and some over the counter pain meds. Since both his bath and the one in the guest suite had jetted tubs, they ended up back here at his place.

With full security engaged.

It still wasn't clear if Chloe's murderer was targeting them, but with this being the third time they were nearly killed, Aiden wasn't taking any chances. Especially since it'd be night soon, and he didn't want anyone trying to sneak up on them and launch a grenade or set off another round of heated-up bullets.

"I'm not sure if the caffeine will actually help," Lexa said, setting one of the Cokes on the kitchen island next to where he was seated. "It might make us even more alert to the aches."

That was likely true, but with both of them battling adrenaline crashes from hell, they needed the caffeine to help them focus on…well, a lot of shit. There were reports coming in about every half hour from the bomb squad as they cleared each area of the grid they'd marked off in the woods. More texts and calls from family and friends, making sure they were all right. They were.

Mostly.

Aiden looked at Lexa to make sure that mostly applied. At that exact second, she looked at him, and their gazes connected. There was a small, bandaged cut on her forehead, a bruise on her cheekbone, and a scratch on her neck.

"If I kissed you now, I'd have to be very careful," he said. And as he'd hoped, that caused her to smile.

"Same for you." Lexa motioned toward the fresh bandage over his stitches. "Is there a part of you that isn't bruised, scraped or cut?" she asked.

"I think my left ass cheek is good. You?"

She smiled again, this time the humor actually making it to her eyes. But he saw something else still there. The heat.

Yep, even now.

Apparently, lust could create grand illusions about what was logistically possible. Of course, kissing, sex, and such were doable, but oh, there'd be some pain until the mindless need totally kicked in and took over.

"My right breast and navel came out unscathed," Lexa let him know.

Even that notched up the heat some, and he got a flash of his tongue playing around with those particular parts of her body. Aiden might have moved in closer to give that a try, but his phone rang.

"It's Owen," Aiden grumbled when he checked the screen. His boss had lousy timing with some things, but this was no doubt important, and it put the lust stuff on hold.

Aiden set his Coke aside and answered the call,

putting it on speaker. "How are you two doing?" their boss immediately wanted to know.

"Good," they said in unison. "We'll try to make it through the night without getting shot at and blown up," Aiden added. "Any news on what caused that blast?"

"Apparently, a rather crudely made IED," Owen replied. "One that could have been built from instructions gotten off the internet."

"So, something Chloe could have likely made herself," Lexa concluded.

"Probably, but there's another possibility. The head of the bomb squad said he got a report of another one nearly identical to this one, and it was used to blow off the reinforced door of a warehouse where a couple of Hummers were being stored. The bomber was caught on a hidden surveillance camera and identified as Travis Walker. He's still at large, but Chloe and he were once an item in high school and have remained friends over the years."

"Hell," Aiden spat out.

"Yeah, that was my reaction, too," Owen went on. "Especially when I learned that Travis has bragged to friends about owning various kinds of explosives. He could have been the one who fired those two grenades." He paused. "Could have also been the one to kill Chloe if something went south in their relationship."

True. And Aiden didn't have to ask if the cops were working hard to find him. They would be.

Travis could hold a lot of answers about this investigation.

"As for the IED by Chloe's car," Owen went on a moment later, "Orville probably set it off by stepping on it."

That'd been Aiden's guess as well, and it twisted at him to know he hadn't been able to stop it. That must have shown on his face because Lexa put her Coke on the counter, reached over and took hold of his left hand. She gave it a gentle squeeze.

And that helped far more than Aiden had even thought it would.

They were kindred spirits on this. Both had survived hell and back ordeals. Both were eaten away with guilt over not being able to save a man's life.

"There's more," Owen said, yanking Aiden's attention back to the call. "We finally have proof that Chloe had contact with her bio-mom. Lots of it, according to one of Chloe's former coworkers. She's been away on vacation so she wasn't interviewed until about a half hour ago. But she verified that Chloe and Silby not only reconnected, but they also saw each other at least once a week."

"Why keep that secret?" Aiden asked.

"According to the coworker, Chloe didn't want to hurt her adoptive parents' family, but apparently Silby and she got quite close. So close that Chloe was devastated when the woman was killed. Then, she was enraged when the drunk driver got off with a slap on the wrist."

Well, that was a confirmed motive for Chloe wanting to get back at Wylie. And if Travis had indeed been the one to kill her from a soured relationship, that could mean the threats were over and that this investigation could come to an end once Travis was captured.

But that felt like wishful thinking on Aiden's part.

"Gotta go," Owen abruptly said. "I need to try to contact Miles again, and I want to find out if he had any contact with Chloe, Hudson or even Travis." With that, he hung up.

Lexa still had hold of Aiden's hand, and she gave it another squeeze before she started to pull back. He stopped her by easing his fingers around hers to keep her from moving away. *Gently easing* because there was the possibility she was in pain there, too.

If she was, she didn't show it.

Just the opposite. Obviously, being careful about his stitched arm, she locked their fingers together and tugged him closer. Not that she had to tug too hard. Aiden was more than eager to go where she was leading him. And where she was leading him was right into her arms.

Yeah, there was some pain when his chest landed against her breasts, but as he'd thought, lust had a way of overriding that. Hell, overriding everything, including common sense. Because there was no way he should be launching into anything with Lexa when they still had so much on their plates.

But here they were.

Chest to breasts. Breath to breath. And a split-second later, mouth to mouth. Since he still had zero chance of resisting her, Aiden just went with it.

He sank right into that kiss. Right into Lexa, their bodies melting against each other. Pain vanished, and the heat came. Mercy, did it. After one taste of her, he was toast.

That taste and heat roared through him and instantly kicked up the need. Oh, he wanted her. Bad. And that want came through in the kiss. He made it long, deep, and hard, all the while drawing her closer and closer to him until they were fitted against each other like the perfect pieces of a sex puzzle.

Well, some parts weren't linked that way yet, and his dick was anxious to remedy that.

Aiden slid his hand, again gently, over her back and down to her butt. He pressed her center to his. And damn near groaned out loud from the slam of pleasure. Thankfully, he kept that particular reaction in his head because a groan would have interrupted the kiss. He wanted this one to go for a long, long time.

Especially since he couldn't let it escalate into sex.

Or rather he *shouldn't* let things go that far.

Aiden silently repeated that to himself several times. But the warning wasn't getting through to his dick.

Lexa eased her mouth from his, dropping back a couple of inches. Her breath was gusting now, causing her breasts to push rhythmically against her shirt. He could see the outline of her nipples, and her face was flushed with arousal. It was damn sexy, and Aiden had to fight not to launch back into another round.

"You're more effective than painkillers," she muttered through that gusting breath. And she laughed.

That was damn sexy, too, and despite, well, everything, he had to smile. Not just because of this heat that still teased around them. Nope. It was more than that. He had kissed her, had had completely raunchy thoughts about her, and hadn't gotten a single flashback of the nightmare they'd shared three years ago.

Or of the most recent nightmares they'd experienced together.

That was progress. And Aiden was thankful for it. He was falling hard for Lexa, and he didn't want their pasts or anything else getting in the way of that.

"Just how bad will we screw things up if this goes any further?" she asked.

Aiden wasn't sure. Nor did he especially want to think about it. He only wanted to think of Lexa. Of this moment. But at least she was showing some restraint.

Or not.

He had to amend that when she reached out, took hold of the front of his shirt and hauled him back to her. Mouth to mouth. Body to body. Yeah, and injury to injury, too, but there was a hell of a lot more pleasure than there was pain.

Aiden tried to keep things gentle. He didn't tighten his uninjured arm around her waist. Not too much anyway. Tried not to do anything that would cause her pain. But Lexa obviously had an opinion about that as well.

"Forget that I'm hurt," she insisted, backing him out of the kitchen and toward the bedroom. "Kiss me the way I think you've been wanting to kiss me. Hard, deep, and holding nothing back. I wouldn't even mind a love bite or two."

Aiden obliged. He didn't hold back. Not one bit. He kissed her as if the injuries didn't exist. As if there were no consequences and no murder investigation. This was a battle now. One to hurl them toward that pleasure. That need.

That release.

Man, he needed that. He needed Lexa.

They kissed and staggered their way into his bedroom, somehow making it to the bed without falling on their asses on the floor. Instead, they fell on their asses on the bed.

Lexa immediately levered herself up and went after his zipper. Her motions were frantic and quick.

"I'm thinking sex now," she said. "Something like the kiss. Fast and thorough. So please tell me you have a condom."

Oh, man. He went as hard as stone, and he reached over to yank open the nightstand drawer. Aiden took out some condoms and tossed them on the bed.

Lexa unzipped him and shoved down his pants and boxers. His erection was there for her to see.

"Yes," she said, nodding. "That's what I want."

Then, they were definitely on the same page. For that anyway. Because Aiden wanted her to want *that*.

He helped her with his holster and boots, but Lexa was clearly on a mission to get him naked. And she managed it just fine. The pants and boxers came off. His tee as well that she eased over his stitched arm. She tossed the clothes on the floor and set his body on fire with some kisses to his chest.

To his stomach.

And, yeah, lower.

The woman was amazing at dealing out the sweet torture. But Aiden knew his body couldn't take much of that, and he wanted them to finish this together. He also wanted her naked, and he did something about that. He rid her of her clothes, tossing them on the floor with his, and his reward for that was having a butt-naked Lexa in his bed.

He looked down to the center of her body. "That's what I want," he said, repeating her words.

"Then, take it," she insisted.

Aiden kissed her mouth, hard. Her breasts, too.

It'd been a while since he'd given a woman a love bite, but he put one on the top of her left breast. Then, her right one. Both earned high praise with some dirty talk and moans and Lexa. He would have attempted one lower if Lexa hadn't latched onto his erection and had him seeing stars.

"We finish this now," she said.

Again, he wasn't about to refuse. He got the condom on, moved her legs apart and slipped inside her.

Oh, hell.

More stars. And he couldn't catch his breath. The sensations slammed through him, as if all the nerves in his body were firing at the same time.

"We finish this now," Lexa repeated.

He didn't have a choice about that either. She lifted her hips, taking his fully inside her. Her head arched back. She moaned. Cursed. Mumbled something about *hard sex.*

Aiden gave her that, too. He had a hard grip on her hips, but she kept shoving herself against him. And her fingers dug into his arms. She met him thrust for thrust.

"We finish this now," she whispered.

And he did. Aiden pushed into her one last time. She came in a flash, her muscles latching onto him and squeezing him to a climax.

We finish this now.

But Aiden had the feeling this finished nothing, that this was just the start.

———— ☆ ————

CHAPTER FIFTEEN

☆

Aiden hadn't intended to doze off, but he had, and when he jolted awake, he realized Lexa had fallen asleep as well.

Good.

They'd both obviously needed some rest, and the sex had certainly helped with that. It'd helped with a lot of things. His body was still beat to hell and back, but the pain had dulled considerably.

Lexa and he were on his bed, naked and wrapped around each other. It'd been the position they'd landed after he'd made a pitstop in his bathroom. The cuddling had felt like the perfect way to end the sex.

And it still felt perfect.

As if she was suddenly aware that he was thinking about her, Lexa stirred, her eyes opening, and she smiled at him. "I'll say it again," she muttered, brushing a lazy kiss on his mouth, "you're better than painkillers. I still have a nice sex buzz."

So did he. And he was thinking about round two. But his ringing phone put a stop to that notion.

Cursing, Aiden got up, located his phone that was on the floor amid their clothes, and he checked the screen. And was surprised at the name he saw there. Not Owen with an update about his call with Miles.

"It's Brady," he told Lexa. "You're on speaker and Lexa's here with me," Aiden let Brady know when he answered the call.

"I heard about the explosion," Brady said. "Are you two all right?"

"Been better," Aiden settled on saying. "How about you?"

He heard Brady's long sigh. "I called to tell Lexa and you how sorry I am."

That put Aiden on full alert. "Why are you apologizing?"

"Because I didn't see Chloe for what she was. I didn't pick up on this plan of hers to stage her own murder and set me up for it." Brady sighed again and followed it with a groan. "I swear, I didn't see it, and I should have. If I had, so much damage wouldn't have been done, and Chloe might be alive to face justice for this nightmare she caused."

There was no sighing now but rather anger in Brady's voice. "I knew Chloe and I didn't see it either," Lexa was quick to point out.

"But her brother probably did," Brady spat out. "I hope Owen will arrest his sorry ass."

"Owen will do just that if there's cause to arrest him," Aiden assured him.

"You don't think he's the one who killed Chloe?" Brady came out and asked.

"It doesn't matter what I think. It only matters what can be proven. This investigation is still ongoing."

And hopefully they'd have a few more answers after Owen finished talking with Miles. If he managed it, that is. Miles' parents could be stonewalling that conversation.

Brady stayed quiet a couple of seconds. "You're right. Sorry for the rant. My head is just whirling with everything. I can't sleep. I can't eat. I can only keep going back to why I trusted her. To why I fell in love with her."

Obviously, Chloe was convincing and damn cold-hearted to have kept up the charade for months.

"There's talk all over town," Brady went on a moment later. "Talk that I helped Chloe try to get back at my dad for helping her mother's killer go free."

Hell. How that got around? But then he thought of all the CSIs and other responders who'd been on the multiple crime scenes. Lots of chances for someone to overhear a conversation. Added to that, those questioned during an interview could have put it together.

"Please tell me that you don't believe I had a part in Chloe's plan," Brady added a heartbeat later.

Aiden hesitated. Not long. But it was there. And Brady picked up on it.

"You do believe it," Brady spat out, and he didn't give Aiden a chance to respond because he cursed and ended the call.

"Great," Aiden grumbled—just as his phone rang again. And this time it was indeed Owen.

"Hudson does have a connection to Miles," Owen blurted the moment Aiden answered on speaker. "Hudson was doing a private bartending gig at a party. Miles and a few of his buddies sneaked in, and Hudson gave them drinks."

Hell in a handbasket. That explained why Chloe was so pissed at her brother. She must have found out what happened.

"When Miles was arrested, he didn't rat Hudson out," Owen added. "He lied and said he got the booze from his parents' house. Miles admitted he said that, thinking his parents might go easier on him if they thought they'd had a part in what happened."

Lexa started picking up her clothes and putting them back on. Since they were obviously shifting to the work mode, Aiden did the same.

"Why did Miles decide to come clean now?" Lexa wanted to know.

"I told him about Chloe's murder, that it could be connected to what happened to her bio-mom, and Miles got scared. He thinks Hudson might try to kill him. I've alerted SAPD so they know the situation, and his parents are arranging for some extra security. Hold on a second," Owen said.

In the background Aiden could hear Owen talking with someone, but he couldn't make out who or what was being said.

"Shit," Owen grumbled several moments later when he came back on the line. "Gillian just made a 911 call. She said someone's broken into her house. And before the operator could ask for any other info, Gillian screamed, and the line went dead."

———— ☆ ————

CHAPTER SIXTEEN

☆

Lexa was sure that Owen wasn't going to approve of Aiden and her showing up at Gillian's, but that hadn't stopped them from rushing out to the cruiser to head that way.

Because Gillian could have met the same fate as Chloe.

Possibly.

Lexa didn't know why the killer would go after Gillian, but she doubted a break-in was a coincidence after everything else that'd happened.

"Stating the obvious here, but this could be a trap," Aiden reminded her as she drove toward Outlaw Ridge. "A trap either set up by Gillian herself or by the person who murdered Chloe."

Yep. It could be. It was possible there was no break in at all and that Gillian's scream and dead phone were all part of a plan to lure the police to her house so she could kill them. But there was that pesky question of motive. If Gillian had been the one who'd killed Chloe, then why try to eliminate any cops? It didn't make sense unless...

"Maybe Gillian or the killer think we're getting too close to solving this case," Lexa spelled out.

"Or they think we saw them," he added. "We did see someone at the manor, but we didn't get a good look at him or her. The killer might not know that. As long as we're alive, there's a chance we could ID the person we saw at the scene."

Again, that was true. And if that had occurred to Owen, then he definitely might not want Aiden and her out and about. But cops couldn't always afford the luxury of staying safe when there was a killer on the loose.

She took the turn toward town, heading now to Main Street, but to the north side, on the outskirts, where there was a new subdivision, Wildflower Bluff, being built. Shortly after she'd moved back here, Lexa had considered buying a place there, but she'd nixed that since there had still been a lot of construction going on. Only about a dozen houses had been finished, and there were more than twenty more slated to be built. She hadn't wanted to deal with the noise.

"Gillian's address is 2220 Bluebell Lane," Aiden told her. "After we're on the main drag of the subdivision, we take the first right, and it's the fourth house on the left."

So, the house was toward the back of the development. Probably not good because it could mean neighbors hadn't seen her or heard what was going on.

Her phone rang, and Owen's name popped up on the dash screen. She used her hands free to accept the call.

"I'm guessing you're on your way to Gillian's," Owen immediately said. "And if you're not, I need you here right away," he added, surprising her. "There's blood and signs of a struggle inside the house, but no Gillian. I want you to search for her because we got other problems, and, yes, that's plural. Someone's put small explosives devices all over town."

"Hell," Aiden muttered. "Have any of them detonated?"

"Not yet, but we need to find them and keep people away from them. Shaw, Declan, Jemma, and Hayes are on that since we don't know how damn many there are. Callie and I are heading to Brady's house. Someone firebombed it, and he says the person ran into the greenbelt behind his property."

Aiden repeated that "hell" along with some other profanity. Lexa had a similar response. This was basically a three-pronged attack of some kind. But who was behind it?

"Get to Gillian's," Owen said. "Find out where she is, and the rest of us will deal with these other shitstorms."

Lexa and Aiden assured him they would as Owen ended the call. She sped up, turning on the blue lights, and the cruiser quickly ate up the distance to Gillian's. She looked for any of those explosive devices along the way but didn't see any.

Maybe the deputies would be able to round up all of them before anyone got hurt. Or killed the way Orville had.

After only a couple of minutes, she spotted the white limestone sign at the entrance to Wildflower Bluff, and while there were lights around it, the neighborhood itself was cloaked in darkness. That was in part due to the lack of streetlights and that nearly every other lot was still vacant.

Following the directions that Aiden had given her, Lexa slowed down, again checking for any possible explosives on or alongside the road. Checking for a killer, too, because all of this could have been orchestrated to set a trap. She thought of the massacre that'd nearly wiped out the police force and prayed that wasn't what the killer had in mind now.

She took the turn onto Bluebell Lane and silently cursed the darkness. It would be hard to spot anyone with only a handful of lights. Added to that, there were mainly unfinished houses here with stacks of construction vehicles and equipment. Plenty of places for someone to hide.

Lexa pulled into the driveway of 2220 Bluebell Lane and got her first look at the one-story stucco house.

And the front door that was wide open.

She figured it'd been like that when Owen and Shaw had arrived, and she wondered if the intruder had left it that way or if Gillian had used it to try to escape. If it was the latter, the woman could be around here somewhere.

"Watch your six," Aiden reminded her, and they both drew their weapons as they stepped from the cruiser.

They didn't linger around outside. No need to make themselves easy targets for a sniper. But eventually, they would have to search the grounds. For now though, they started with the house.

Lexa didn't see any blood on the porch, but she did the moment Aiden and she stepped inside. There were some drops on the white tiled floor of the foyer.

"Gillian?" Lexa called out.

No response. And she couldn't hear anyone moving around.

Aiden and she moved together, slowly and with lots of caution while they began to check the open-plan living, dining, and kitchen. Owen had been right about there being signs of a struggle. The lamp had been knocked off the end table, and there was a shattered wine glass next to it.

Lexa nearly gasped when there was a sharp beeping sound in the kitchen area, and with their guns aimed, they pivoted in that direction. It took her a second to realize it was the microwave. The light was flashing "Ready" on it, and she guessed Gillian had put something in to cook before she'd heard the intruder.

If that story was true.

Lexa reminded herself again that Gillian might

have staged this the way Chloe had done at the manor. The woman could be lying in wait to try to kill them.

"Gillian?" she tried again as they made their way through the other rooms.

Still, no answer, and there were no signs of a struggle in the main bedroom and bath. Ditto for the powder room in the hall. Aiden and she searched them, looking in every possible hiding spot.

No Gillian.

There were two more rooms off the hall, both with their doors shut, and Aiden and she made their way to them. He took the right side. Lexa took the left. When Aiden threw open the door, he immediately flicked on the lights. Nothing out of the ordinary here. It appeared to be a guest room, and everything seemed to be intact so they moved to the next one, repeating the same maneuver as they entered a home office.

This time though when Aiden turned on the lights, they saw something that definitely qualified as *out of the ordinary*. There were dozens, maybe hundreds of photos pinned to the walls.

Of Brady.

A few were shots with Gillian and him, but most were of Brady solo. Lexa recognized some of the other pictures as being printed out from social media and the town's newspaper, but others appeared to have been taken with a long-range camera lens. In some of them, Brady didn't seem to be aware that he was being photographed.

None of the photos included Chloe.

In addition to the pictures, there were framed articles detailing all of Brady's military accomplishments, his wins when he'd been the quarterback of the high school football team, and even his graduation from college.

"Shit, she's obsessed with Brady," Aiden murmured.

Lexa agreed. No way was this normal. Gillian had basically been stalking Brady, and judging from these photos and printouts, it'd been going on for years. She had always known that Gillian had a thing for Brady, but she hadn't imagined the woman taking it this far.

But had Gillian done even more than this?

She could have murdered Chloe to make sure she was out of Brady's life.

Something else caught Lexa's eye when she looked at the trash can. There, on top of some other garbage, were torn-up bits of paper, and there was enough of it left for Lexa to recognize what it was.

An invitation for Brady and Chloe's wedding.

"Hell. That's not good," Aiden said, and she followed his gaze to a small table tucked to the side of the desk. "That's a detonator for an explosive."

That got them moving, fast, and they hurried out of the hall and to the front door. Lexa hadn't noticed any actual explosives attached to the device, but that didn't mean there wasn't some in the house.

"Let's get in the cruiser," Aiden suggested. "We can call the bomb squad, let Owen know what we've found, and then drive around and look for Gillian."

That sounded like a good plan to her, and she didn't waste any time dashing out of the house and back into the car. "I'll call Owen. You deal with the bomb squad," she said though both were no doubt tied up with looking for those explosives. Still, they had to know.

Lexa made the call to Owen, and he answered on the first ring. "There's a detonator in Gillian's house," she blurted.

"Shit, how did I miss that? Never mind. I was in and out because of the call I got about the explosive device, but I'll get somebody over there now. Any sign of Gillian?" he tacked onto that.

She was about to say no, but then she caught some movement from the corner of her eye. Lexa's head snapped in that direction, and in the dim moonlight, she spotted someone.

Gillian.

She was by the side of a Dumpster filled with construction debris that sat on the edge of an empty lot. Behind her was a partially finished house, and to her left was a heavily treed lot that hadn't yet been cleared.

It was hard to tell, but it appeared as if the front of her dress was covered in blood.

Gillian looked at the cruiser, and for a moment,

Lexa thought the woman was about to head their way. Then, Gillian glanced back over her shoulder. Back into that shell of a house.

And she screamed.

Before she started running straight toward the trees.

———————— ☆ ————————

CHAPTER SEVENTEEN

Damn it all to hell. This was not how Aiden had wanted this to play out. Not with Lexa and he sprinting toward Gillian. But here they were—doing just that.

And maybe running straight into a deadly trap.

He thought of the blood they'd seen on Chloe's wedding dress. Blood that the woman had almost certainly put there herself to make people think she'd been seriously injured or even murdered. Well, Gillian could be doing that. She could have soaked her shirt with blood, or the fake stuff, all so she could lure Lexa and him to her. And then try to kill them.

But they couldn't just stay put.

Not with both Lexa and him being cops. Because if Gillian was truly injured and being chased by a killer, then they had to help her. They had to stop her from being murdered.

Because his legs were longer than Lexa's, Aiden could have easily outrun her, but there was no way he wanted to leave her behind and dash into those trees. That could make it easier for someone to try to pick her off. Or, hell, pick him off as well. It was a necessity they stay together.

Ahead of them, he heard Gillian scream again. A blood-curdling shriek that cranked up his adrenaline and sent his heart racing. Because he'd heard screams like that before.

And that situation had not turned out well. Now, he only hoped the flashbacks didn't get to both Lexa and him. They needed to stay sharp. Focused. Because it sure seemed that Gillian was trying to escape someone who terrified her.

Lexa and he kept moving, fast, and when they reached the Dumpster where they'd first seen Gillian, they ducked to the side of it. Not ideal cover, but it was better than nothing.

Their breaths were both gusting, and it was hard to hear over the pulse jackhammering away in his ears. But they stood there, listening for any sound to let them know where Gillian was.

Nothing.

Not at first anyway.

Then, Aiden heard some rustling in the trees. The night and the thick branches of the oaks made it impossible to see anyone moving around, but someone was in there. Maybe just Gillian. And if a killer was indeed after her, Aiden hoped she had found a hiding place and would stay quiet.

"I need to text Owen," Lexa whispered, taking out her phone.

While she did that, Aiden kept watch around them. Kept listening, too. But he saw or heard nothing. He didn't want to risk calling out to Gillian because if the woman answered, it could give away her position.

Of course, she might already be dead.

And if so, then the killer could already be escaping.

Aiden wasn't that familiar with this subdivision, but the odds were there was a road not far behind those trees. It could have been where Gillian's intruder had parked.

The questions came. Why was this happening? And who was behind it? But Aiden had to shove that aside. Right now, Lexa and he had to try to find Gillian.

She finished the text to Owen, put her phone away and tipped her head to the trees. "Are you ready to go in there?" she muttered.

No, he wasn't. He hated putting Lexa at risk like this, but it occurred to him that she might feel the same way about him. She was a veteran cop after all, and they had both faced danger. Had both been bitten in the proverbial ass, too, by a rescue mission gone wrong. That didn't change things.

No.

And with a nod, Lexa and he got moving again.

Together and with their guns ready, they raced to the edge of the partially constructed house. Again, it wasn't ideal cover, but they didn't stay there long, only a couple of seconds, before they hurried to the first tree. They darted behind it and paused to listen.

Again, he didn't hear anything.

Aiden tried to pick through the darkness to try to see Gillian or anyone else, and he caught just a blur of motion. Maybe the breeze teasing a branch on one of the trees. But it was movement all right.

He pointed out the area to Lexa and focused on it while his eyes continued to adjust to the night.

And he saw it again.

Maybe someone crouched down? It was impossible to tell from this angle so he motioned for Lexa to move. They did, hurrying to the next tree before they pulled up again.

This new position put them closer to that shadow but not close enough so they had to do the maneuver again. And again. Each step took them closer until he could finally make out the person.

Gillian.

She was hunkered down, her back pressed to a large tree trunk. The woman wasn't moving, and the way she was positioned, Aiden couldn't tell if she was even breathing. She could be dead.

Lexa looked at him, their gazes connecting for just a second, and he knew with that look, she was going in. So was he, even though they both knew the risk they were taking. They bolted off from cover, heading straight to Gillian.

The woman moved then, her head whipping in their direction. So, she was alive. Maybe ready to kill them.

But Aiden didn't see her lift a gun or any other weapon.

Still, that didn't mean Gillian didn't have one tucked on the other side of her body. Or she hadn't planted some kind of boobytraps, maybe one of those IEDs that had been scattered around town.

"Run!" Gillian shouted.

Just as the gunshot blasted through the air.

Aiden took hold of Lexa's arm, pulling her down, but she had already started in that direction. They landed on the ground on top of some dead leaves, rocks, and twigs, and the moment Aiden caught his breath, his gaze fired around, looking for their attacker.

The shot hadn't come from Gillian. He was certain of that. His gaze had been pinned on her when the blast had happened.

Another shot came, this one slamming into the tree right over Gillian's head. She screamed again and started scrambling away, crawling toward Lexa and him.

Aiden rolled to the side, searching for the shooter. He still couldn't see him, but that second shot had given him an idea of where the gunman was. To the right, no doubt behind one of the trees.

Lexa cursed. "We can't return fire," she whispered.

No, they couldn't. Because there were houses nearby which meant they couldn't just start shooting because they could end up killing an innocent bystander.

If Aiden had been alone and if Gillian hadn't been here, still screaming for help, he would have tried to circle around and come up behind the shooter. For now though, the priority had to be Gillian. Yeah, she could be faking this, but she could also be on the verge of being murdered.

Another shot blasted out. Again, aimed at Gillian. Or rather in her direction anyway. It slammed into the ground, kicking up dirt and debris.

"Try to cover me," he told Lexa, and that was the only warning he gave her before he moved.

Aiden stayed low, automatically taking aim in the direction of the shooter, and he raced toward Gillian. He latched onto the woman's arm and started dragging her toward one of the larger trees.

The shooter fired again.

The shot missed both of them, but Aiden could have sworn he felt the heat coming off the bullet. That one, too, blasted into the ground.

The next shot didn't.

It came right at them, and Aiden heard the sickening sound of a bullet thudding into flesh. Not his. He wasn't shot.

But Gillian was.

Aiden felt the spray of warm blood hit his face, and a strangled gasp clawed its way past Gillian's throat. She muttered something, garbled sounds he didn't understand. But he did understand that he had to get them both out of the line of fire. It was their only chance of surviving this.

He scooped her up, hauling her behind the tree, and then he immediately looked in Lexa's direction. Aiden couldn't see her, and he hoped like hell that she stayed behind cover.

Another shot rang out, this one tearing off a huge chunk of the tree right next to Aiden's head. He dropped down lower, trying to figure out where Gillian had been shot so he could maybe apply pressure to the wound. That might stop her from bleeding out since an ambulance wouldn't be able to get in here as long as there was active gunfire.

He soon learned that Gillian had plenty of blood on her. On the front of her shirt, her shoulder, and leg. On the side of her head, too. Aiden couldn't tell though where the actual injuries were, but one thing was for certain, she wasn't faking these injuries. Those moans of pain were the real deal, and her breathing was way too shallow. He could practically feel her dying in his arms.

Shit.

The flashbacks came, but cursing them, Aiden fought them. Fought them hard and continued to feel around until he located a bullet wound. Right on Gillian's stomach. Yeah, she was bleeding out all right, and Aiden decided the best way to help her was to stop the son of a bitch who was shooting at them so the EMTs could get in here and try to save her.

"You coward," Aiden shouted, hoping to taunt the shooter. "Too much of a coward to show your face."

And he wondered whose face it was. Wylie's? Hudson's? Brady's. Of those three, he could easily see Hudson doing this. Or rather he wanted it to be Hudson. Because if it was Wylie or Brady, it meant someone he knew well was a killer.

Well, maybe.

There was another possible player in this. Travis Walker, the man who'd likely built the IEDs. He could be doing mop-up for Chloe.

But that didn't feel right.

A hired thug would be more likely to try to stay hidden away rather than come at them like this. That thought had barely crossed his mind when Aiden heard something. Not a gasp but some shuffling movement.

Sounds of a struggle.

"Lexa," he managed to say, already getting up to rush to her.

But he was already too late.

Aiden bolted from the tree to see Lexa. Not alone. Someone was behind her, and while Aiden couldn't see the person's face, Lexa's captor had a gun pressed to her head.

---- ☆ ----

CHAPTER EIGHTEEN

———— ☆ ————

Lexa cursed herself for not moving faster. For not getting fully turned around before someone grabbed her from behind. Hard. The person knocked her Glock out of her hand, locked an arm around her throat, and put a gun to her right temple.

"Fight me, and I blow your brains out," the man snarled in a whisper with his mouth right against her ear.

Brady.

Oh, God. It was Brady.

She had to fight through the shock of that. Had to try to wrap her mind around it. But that was next to impossible. A man she'd known most of her life was now threatening to kill her.

Her mind began to whirl as she tried to piece together what was happening. And what had already happened that had brought them here, to this nightmare.

"Call out to Aiden," Brady demanded, still

whispering.

Lexa looked in the spot where she'd last seen Aiden. But he wasn't there. And she couldn't see Gillian either. Aiden had no doubt moved back behind cover with the woman. Good. Because if Brady had been the one to shoot Gillian, then he might try to finish her off.

"Why do you want me to call out to Aiden?" Lexa snapped.

"Because do it or you're dead," Brady replied. His voice was a hoarse tangle of nerves and something else. Fear. She could hear it. Feel it. "Make it fast before your backup arrives, or a whole lot of people are going to have to die."

Every muscle in her body had already tightened, but that vised them even more. "You plan on killing Aiden and me. Why?" she repeated.

"Shout for Aiden to come to you," Brady snarled, and this time there was raw anger mixed with the fear in that whisper.

So, Brady wanted her to help him kill Aiden. That was *not* going to happen.

"No," Lexa replied.

She was well aware that she was dealing with a former Navy SEAL, someone who'd been trained to kill. He could snap her neck with the fierce chokehold he had on her. But Lexa hoped he realized if she was dead, then she couldn't be used to lure out Aiden. He would lose his leverage.

Brady cursed, and Lexa could feel him stoop down even lower behind her than he already was.

Using her as a shield. Aiden had been right to call him a coward though at the time he'd said that, he likely hadn't known the coward was Brady.

"Do it," Brady demanded, jamming the gun so hard against her temple that Lexa nearly yelped in pain. "Call out for Aiden."

She forced herself not to react. Not to make a sound. Because Aiden would no doubt try to save her.

That thought repeated in her head. No way would Aiden have gone this long without at least glancing out at her. So, where was he? She was dead sure he wasn't just laying low to protect himself.

No.

He was coming for her.

And she needed to help him. To make sure Aiden got to Brady before Brady could kill them.

"Chloe deserved to die," she said. That wasn't true, but she wanted the sound of her voice to cover any movement that Aiden might make.

"Damn right she did," Brady spat out, the rage building now. He was moving, too, shifting his feet and dragging her right along with him while he tried to keep watch around them. "That fucking bitch. She was going to set me up for her murder."

"Yes," Lexa agreed. "And that's why no one is grieving her death."

"No one except her brother. I overheard Chloe talking with him a couple of days ago. She wanted Hudson to help her with this sick plan, but he refused."

Days. Brady had known about Chloe's plan all this time. Which means he could have gone to the cops to stop it. Apparently though, he'd decided to handle the situation himself. And look where that had gotten them.

"Hudson did something right for once by turning her down," Brady added. "But that's when I knew Chloe was going to pay and pay hard."

Lexa thought she heard some movement behind them, and she quickly tried to cover it with her voice. "Someone else helped Chloe. The guy who built the IEDs and maybe helped her set those cook-off fires. He needs to be arrested. You need to help us find him."

"Travis," Brady spat out like venom. "Yeah, I learned about him, too, by planting bugs in Chloe's car and house. He's already paid. He's dead."

"You killed him after he set the IEDs here in town for you," she said, though Lexa was almost sure that wasn't true.

It wasn't.

Brady huffed. "I wouldn't have trusted that asshole to set them up. I had to have a distraction, and the IEDs gave me one. Minimum collateral damage. That's what I want here."

Minimum collateral damage. In other words, Brady intended to kill only those who knew he had murdered Chloe. But Aiden and she hadn't known. Not until now.

"You thought Aiden and I saw you at the

manor," she muttered.

"You did see me. Or at least Aiden did. I'm sure of it. And the only reason he didn't arrest me was because he's my friend. He didn't want to believe I'd set that fire. But I hadn't intended that fire to kill the two of you. That was all for Chloe, but I guess she'd gotten out right before Aiden and you arrived."

It was little comfort to her to know they hadn't been the targets. Because Brady's careless actions, combined with Chloe's, could have gotten a lot of people killed. Heck, it had killed Orville.

"And Chloe's car?" she asked.

"Not my doing. Chloe's," he insisted. "Or rather Travis'. I'm sure she had him set that up for her."

There was sound behind them. Brady suddenly pivoted around, keeping her anchored in front of him. Keeping the gun to her head.

Aiden.

He was there, only about ten feet away behind a tree.

"Brady, you don't want to do this," Aiden said, and in the distance, Lexa heard the howl of police sirens.

"The hell, I don't. I'm saving myself here," Brady argued. "Is Gillian dead?" he tacked onto that.

"No. She's alive and talking," Aiden replied. Lexa had no idea if that was the truth. "She told me what you did to her."

"She shouldn't have played detective," Brady

ranted, the rage back in his voice. He tightened his arm around her throat, and Lexa had to fight for air. "And she got it all wrong. She called me to say that she was certain my dad had killed Chloe. My dad! He had nothing to do with this shit."

"Ease up on your chokehold," Aiden warned him. "If Lexa passes out, she'll drop down, and you'll be an easy kill. Then, you'll never get the chance to finish off Gillian or me."

Brady cursed. But he did pull back his arm a little. "Gillian's batshit. So, whatever she told you was batshit, too. She said she was going to prove my dad was guilty so that the cops would leave me alone. And so that she and I could be together. I don't want to be with that clingy bitch."

"So, you decided that you had to silence her for good," Aiden finished for him. "You broke into her house to try to make it look like a botched robbery, but she got away."

"Not for long," Brady growled, making a quick glance at the street where that cruiser would soon be arriving. "I have to finish this. No one else needs to die."

"No one except Lexa, Gillian, and me." Aiden's voice wasn't filled with hot rage but rather an icy fury that coated his words and his face. "If you had just believed I was innocent, we wouldn't be here."

"I did believe it," Aiden said.

"Right," Brady answered with a ton of sarcasm. When we talked on the phone, I said, *Please tell me that you don't believe I had a part in Chloe's plan.* You hesitated. And that's when I was certain that you knew what I'd done."

Without warning, Brady shifted his gun away from Lexa's head and took aim at Aiden. He fired, the shot slamming into the tree.

Lexa didn't waste a second. Without his gun on her, she rammed her elbow into Brady's gut, and then pivoting, she punched him in the throat. He howled and staggered back.

But he also lifted his gun.

Pointing it at her.

The blast came, thundering through the air, and Lexa braced herself for the pain. For the sensation of being shot. That didn't happen.

Because Brady hadn't fired the shot.

Aiden had.

And it'd hit Brady right between the eyes.

Brady's face registered just a split-second of shock and then...nothing. His eyes went blank, there was a rattle of breath as it left his now lifeless body. Then, Brady dropped to the ground.

Dead.

---- ☆ ----

CHAPTER NINETEEN

———— ☆ ————

One Week Later

Aiden watched the sunrise from the wall of windows in his bedroom. There was a mist hovering over the pastures, and the sky was a smear of a lot of different colors. Despite what had happened with Brady and the attacks, everything felt peaceful and beautiful.

That included the sleeping woman next to him in bed.

Lexa had her head on his shoulder, her hand on his chest, and her right leg slung over his stomach. Since both of them were naked, that peacefulness would likely soon be replaced with a hefty amount of lust. Then again, any time he was around Lexa, there was lust.

And more.

So much more.

Aiden wasn't sure when or how it'd happened, but he'd fallen head over heels in love with her. His feelings for Lexa had zoomed right past the fierce attraction stage and taken what he considered the ultimate leap. It terrified him and gave him a weird sense of contentment all at the same time. It was as if he'd finally found a missing piece of himself. A piece he hadn't known was missing.

Now, the question was—what was he going to do about it?

Lexa and he had spent a lot of time together since Brady's death. In fact, they'd spent nearly every second together. First, with the aftermath of the investigation and dealing with Brady's death.

What a gut-punch nightmare that had been.

They'd both grieved but not for Brady's death. There had been no choice but to stop him, and that had meant killing him. But the grief had been for not knowing the man, the friend, they thought they had known. For not realizing his plan sooner so they could stop him before so much damage had been done.

Aiden figured Lexa and he would be dealing with that aftermath for the rest of their lives. But at least they were alive. And hopefully they'd get past what'd happened.

Owen had helped with the "getting past" stuff by insisting Lexa and he take some downtime. They had snapped up that offer since it was downtime very much needed. Lexa hadn't actually moved in, but she'd been right here at his place for the entire time.

They'd gotten so damn lucky. Brady could

have, and nearly had, killed both of them. He'd nearly succeeded, too, in murdering Gillian, but she'd had some of that luck as well and was expected to make a full recovery.

Physically anyway.

The trauma would no doubt stay with her for the rest of her life. It was the same for Wylie and Hudson. One had lost a son and the other a sister, and there was absolutely no proof that either of them had helped Chloe or Brady in any way.

No, all the blame for this fell on Chloe for trying to set up Brady and on Brady for trying to punish her for that. The punishment had led to a coverup that had put a lot of innocent people in danger.

The town had also gotten lucky. The bomb squad had managed to locate and disarm all the IEDs that Brady had set. So, Brady hadn't managed to claim any lives with that twisted ploy, but the attempt had led Owen to put some new security measures in place. There were now cameras being installed at all the traffic lights and around the entire perimeter of the police station.

At the thought of Owen and the police station, Aiden glanced over at the nightstand where he'd put his holster and badge. Some of that sunlight glinted off the metal as if spotlighting it. No need for that though. Along with Lexa and Brady, the badge had been on Aiden's mind. Soon, he would need to make a decision as to whether or not to turn it in and resume his job at Strike Force.

Or keep it.

Lexa stirred, making a soft moaning sound, and he looked down at her as she opened those amazing blue eyes. Of course, as far as he was concerned, everything about her fell into that amazing category.

She smiled, took hold of his jaw and tugged him down for a kiss. Not that she had to tug too hard. He was heading there. Along with his feelings for her, Aiden had discovered he looked forward to that first kiss each morning.

And the second one wasn't too shabby either.

It was slow and easy, but it still packed a punch and sent his blood and body revving.

"I want to keep you," he murmured. *Shit*. That came out wrong. "Not in as possessive, creepy kind of way," he added.

She laughed. Kissed him again. And while he loved that kiss, he didn't want her to think of this as a joke. He sank into the kiss for several moments. Then, went with a third kiss before he spoke again.

"When you look at me, do you see the past? The nightmares?" Aiden had to ask.

She kept her gaze locked with his and shook her head. "No, just no. When I look at you, I see a really hot guy. One with an amazing body. I'm talking about a body that could be June or July in one of those hot guy calendars."

Now, he smiled and was glad that she liked what she saw. "Why those months?" he wanted to know.

"Too hot for clothes so a lot of skin showing."

She chuckled and went in for kiss number four. That was longer than some of their foreplays lasted. With Lexa and him, they usually went from a kiss or two—or hell even a look—to full-throttle sex.

"I don't want to give you up," he tried again. In hindsight, he should have rehearsed this.

Another smile. Another kiss. "I'm right here," she assured him.

"I want more," Aiden risked saying. And it was indeed a risk. If Lexa wasn't ready to hear this, then she might slip away from him.

Her right eyebrow winged up. "Are you talking this?" She ran her hand over his dick.

Once he got his eyes uncrossed, he nodded. "That, yes. But more." And he hoped that brainless erection of his held off while he finished telling Lexa what he needed to say.

"More?" she questioned, still playing around with his dick. Feathery light brushes with her very clever fingers.

Somehow, he managed to tip his head to the badge. "For starters, I want to stay a cop. Are you all right with that?"

Her eyes went bright. Her smile deepened. "Absolutely. And I think Owen will be pleased, too."

Owen would be. Aiden had already run the possibility of it past his boss, and while Owen didn't intend to remain sheriff, he was glad that some of his Strike Force operatives were making their temporary positions permanent. Like most people in Outlaw Ridge, Owen only wanted the best for the police department.

"I also want you," he added, but then quickly amended that. Or rather he tried, but Lexa pressed a kiss to his mouth.

"Good," she said when she eased back. "Because, Aiden, I'm head over heels in love with you. I don't want to go anywhere else. I don't want to be with anyone else. I only want you to love me in return. And if it's too soon, I'll back off—"

He kissed her before she could finish that, and because he was suddenly feeling a mountain of relief, and arousal, Aiden rolled over on top of her.

"No backing off," he assured her. "In fact, I want you to say it again. The *I love you* part," he clarified.

Her smile lit up her face even more. "I will if you will," she said like a challenge.

But it was no challenge for him. Apparently, not for Lexa either. Because they said it together.

"I love you."

There it was. The words he'd never grow tired of hearing.

"Know what will make this even more perfect?" he asked.

She smiled, fumbled around the nightstand drawer and managed to take out a condom. "Sex," she murmured, putting the condom on him. "Then, tacos followed by more sex."

Aiden couldn't help it. He laughed. Yeah, Lexa

got him all right, and it was just the beginning. The beginning of those words. And everything else that Lexa and he had started together.

─────── ☆ ───────

ABOUT THE HARD JUSTICE OUTLAW RIDGE SERIES:

The Strike Force team members are former military and cops who assist law enforcement in cold cases and hot investigations where lives are on the line. Their specialty is rescuing kidnapped victims, tracking down killers and protecting those in the path of danger. Strike Force is known for doing what it does best--delivering some hard justice.

ABOUT THE AUTHOR:

Former Air Force Captain Delores Fossen is a New York Times, USA Today, Amazon and Publisher's Weekly bestselling author of over 170 books. She's received the Booksellers Best Award for Best Romantic Suspense and the Romantic Times Reviewers Choice Award. In addition, she's had nearly a hundred short stories and articles published in national magazines. You can contact the author through her webpage at www.deloresfossen.com.

HARD JUSTICE, TEXAS SERIES BOOKS BY DELORES FOSSEN:

Lone Star Rescue (book 1)

Lone Star Showdown (book 2)

Lone Star Payback (book 3)

Lone Star Protector (book 4)

Lone Star Witness (book 5)

Lone Star Target (book 6)

Lone Star Secrets (book 7)

Lone Star Hostage (book 8)

Lone Star Redemption (book 9)

Lone Star Christmas Mission (Novella)

OUTLAW RIDGE: AIDEN

★☆★

HARD JUSTICE: OUTLAW RIDGE SERIES

HAYES (Book 1)
NICO (Book 2)
AIDEN (Book 3)
DECLAN (Book 4)
SHAW Book 5)
REED (Book 6)
JESSE (Book 7)

OTHER BOOKS BY DELORES FOSSEN:

Appaloosa Pass Ranch
1 - Lone Wolf Lawman (Nov-2015)
2 - Taking Aim at the Sheriff (Dec-2015)
3 - Trouble with a Badge (Apr-2016)
4 - The Marshal's Justice (May-2016)
5 - Six-Gun Showdown (Aug-2016)
6 - Laying Down the Law (Sep-2016)

Blue River Ranch
1 - Always a Lawman (Dec-2017)
2 - Gunfire on the Ranch (Jan-2018)
3 - Lawman From Her Past (Mar-2018)
4 - Roughshod Justice (Apr-2018)

Coldwater, Texas
1 - Lone Star Christmas (Sep-2018)
1.5 - Lone Star Midnight (Jan-2019)
2 - Hot Texas Sunrise (Mar-2019)
2.5 - Texas at Dusk (Jun-2019)
3 - Sweet Summer Sunset (Jun-2019)
4 - A Coldwater Christmas (Sep-2019)

Cowboy Brothers in Arms
1 - Heart Like a Cowboy (Dec-2023)
2 - Always a Maverick (May-2024)
3 – Cowboying Up (working title) 2024

Five Alarm Babies
1 - Undercover Daddy (May-2007)
2 - Stork Alert // Whose Baby? (Aug-2007)
3 - The Christmas Clue (Nov-2007)
4 - Newborn Conspiracy (Feb-2008)
5 - The Horseman's Son // The Cowboy's Son (Mar-2008)

Last Ride, Texas

1 - Spring at Saddle Run (May-2021)
2 - Christmas at Colts Creek (Nov-2021)
3 - Summer at Stallion Ridge (Apr-2022)
3.5 - Second Chance at Silver Springs (Oct-2022)
4 - Mornings at River's End Ranch (Dec-2022)
4.5 - Breaking Rules at Nightfall Ranch (Feb-2023)
5 - A Texas Kind of Cowboy (Mar-2023)
6 - Twilight at Wild Springs (Jul-2023)

The Law in Lubbock County
1 - Sheriff in the Saddle (Jul-2022)
2 - Maverick Justice (Aug-2022)
3 - Lawman to the Core (Jan-2023)
4 - Spurred to Justice (Jan-2023)

The Lawmen of Silver Creek Ranch
1 - Grayson (Nov-2011)
2 - Dade (Dec-2011)
3 - Nate (Jan-2012)
4 - Kade (Jul-2012)
5 - Gage (Aug-2012)
6 - Mason (Sep-2012)
7 - Josh (Apr-2014)
8 - Sawyer (May-2014)

9 - Landon (Nov-2016)
10 - Holden (Mar-2017)
11 - Drury (Apr-2017)
12 - Lucas (May-2017)

The Lawmen of McCall Canyon
1 - Cowboy Above the Law (Aug-2018)
2 - Finger on the Trigger (Sep-2018)
3 - Lawman with a Cause (Jan-2019)
4 - Under The Cowboy's Protection (Feb-2019)

Lone Star Ridge
1 - Tangled Up in Texas (Feb-2020)
1.5 - That Night in Texas (May-2020)
2 - Chasing Trouble in Texas (Jun-2020)
2.5 - Hot Summer in Texas (Sep-2020)
3 - Wild Nights in Texas (Oct-2020)
3.5 - Whatever Happens in Texas (Jan-2021)
4 - Tempting in Texas (Feb-2021)
5 - Corralled in Texas (Mar-2022)

Longview Ridge Ranch
1 - Safety Breach (Dec-2019)

2 - A Threat to His Family (Jan-2020)
3 - Settling an Old Score (Aug-2020)
4 - His Brand of Justice (Sep-2020)

The Marshals of Maverick County
1 - The Marshal's Hostage (May-2013)
2 - One Night Standoff (Jun-2013)
3 - Outlaw Lawman (Jul-2013)
4 - Renegade Guardian (Nov-2013)
5 - Justice Is Coming (Dec-2013)
6 - Wanted (Jan-2014)

McCord Brothers
0.5 - What Happens on the Ranch (Jan-2016)
1 - Texas on My Mind (Feb-2016)
1.5 - Cowboy Trouble (May-2016)
2 - Lone Star Nights (Jun-2016)
2.5 - Cowboy Underneath It All (Aug-2016)
3 - Blame It on the Cowboy (Oct-2016)

Mercy Ridge Lawmen
1 - Her Child to Protect (May-2021)
2 - Safeguarding the Surrogate (Jul-2021)

3 - Targeting the Deputy (Dec-2021)

4 - Pursued by the Sheriff (Jan-2022)

Mustang Ridge

1 - Christmas Rescue at Mustang Ridge (Dec-2012)

2 - Standoff at Mustang Ridge (Jan-2013)

Silver Creek Lawmen: Second Generation

1 - Targeted in Silver Creek (Jul-2023)

2 - Maverick Detective Dad (Aug-2023)

3 - Last Seen in Silver Creek (Sep-2023)

4 - Marked For Revenge (Oct-2023)

Sweetwater Ranch

1 - Maverick Sheriff (Sep-2014)

2 - Cowboy Behind the Badge (Oct-2014)

3 - Rustling Up Trouble (Nov-2014)

4 - Kidnapping in Kendall County (Dec-2014)

5 - The Deputy's Redemption (Mar-2015)

6 - Reining in Justice (Apr-2015)

7 - Surrendering to the Sheriff (Jul-2015)

8 - A Lawman's Justice (Aug-2015)

Texas Maternity Hostages
1 - The Baby's Guardian (May-2010)
2 - Daddy Devastating (Jun-2010)
3 - The Mommy Mystery (Jul-2010)

Texas Maternity: Labor and Delivery
1 - Savior in the Saddle (Nov-2010)
2 - Wild Stallion (Dec-2010)
3 - The Texas Lawman's Last Stand (Jan-2011)

Texas Paternity
1 - Security Blanket (Oct-2008)
2 - Branded By The Sheriff (Jan-2009)
3 - Expecting Trouble (Feb-2009)
4 - Secret Delivery (Mar-2009)
5 - Christmas Guardian (Oct-2009)

A Wrangler's Creek Novel
1 - Those Texas Nights (Jan-2017)
2 - No Getting Over a Cowboy (Apr-2017)
3 - Branded as Trouble (Jul-2017)

4 - Lone Star Cowboy (Nov-2016)
5 - One Good Cowboy (Feb-2017)
6 - Just Like a Cowboy (May-2017)
7 - Texas-Sized Trouble (Jan-2018)
8 - Lone Star Blues (Apr-2018)
9 - The Last Rodeo (Jul-2018)
10 - Cowboy Dreaming (Dec-2017)
11 - Cowboy Heartbreaker (Mar-2018)
12 - Cowboy Blues (May-2018)

Daddy Corps
G.I. Cowboy (Apr-2011)

Ice Lake
Cold Heat (Jan-2012)

Kenner County Crime Unit
She's Positive (Jul-2009)

Men on a Mission
Marching Orders (Mar-2003)

Shivers
20 - His to Possess (Oct-2014)

The Silver Star of Texas

Trace Evidence In Tarrant County // For Justice and Love (Feb-2007)

Questioning The Heiress (Jul-2008)

Shotgun Sheriff (Feb-2010)

Top Secret Babies

Mommy Under Cover (Feb-2005)

Printed in Great Britain
by Amazon